Murderously Sweet
A Pumpkin Hollow Mystery
by
Kate Bell

Other books by Kate Bell
Apple Pie A La Murder,
A Cozy Baked Murder, Book 1
Trick or Treat and Murder,
A Cozy Baked Murder, Book 2
Thankfully Dead
A Cozy Baked Murder, Book 3
Candy Cane Killer
A Cozy Baked Murder, Book 4
Ice Cold Murder
A Cozy Baked Murder, Book 5
Love is Murder
A Cozy Baked Murder, Book 6
Strawberry Surprise Killer
A Cozy Baked Murder, Book 7

Pushing Up Daisies in Grady,
A Gracie Williams Mystery, Book 1
Kicked the Bucket in Grady,
A Gracie Williams Mystery, Book 2
Candy Coated Murder
A Pumpkin Hollow Mystery, Book 1
Murderously Sweet
A Pumpkin Hollow Mystery, Book 2

Books by Kathleen Suzette
Clam Chowder and a Murder
A Rainey Daye Cozy Mystery, book 1
Short Stack and a Murder
A Rainey Daye Cozy Mystery, book 2

Table of Contents

Chapter One

"Let the murders begin!"

My head jerked around to see who had shouted. Two teenagers ran toward the entrance to the corn maze, laughing and screaming. I smiled and breathed in deeply. Everything was fine. Hazel Martin's killer was behind bars and the Halloween season would go on as planned.

"You aren't scared of a little corn maze, are you?" a voice said close to my ear.

I squealed and jumped, spinning around to face whoever had spoken.

"Ethan!" I exclaimed. My hair blew across my face and I tucked it back behind my ear.

"Whoa. Sorry, I didn't mean to scare you," he said, holding the flat of his palms toward me. "Sorry, Mia." He grinned as he said it, making me think he didn't mean it.

I rolled my eyes. "Thanks a lot, Ethan. My blood pressure just shot through the roof."

He grinned. "Scaredy cat."

"I am not scared, Mr. Police Officer. I was just taking in a lovely sight," I said, motioning to all the people wandering around the haunted farmhouse with its two frighteningly fun mazes. The three horse-drawn hayrides were just pulling away from the barn and were filled to capacity. "Isn't it lovely?"

"It certainly is," he agreed, looking toward the mazes.

The haunted farmhouse was one of the most popular attractions Pumpkin Hollow had to offer. The tamer maze was made of bales of straw that boasted wooden pumpkin and ghost cutouts. It was well loved by families with small children.

The not so tame maze was made from cornstalks. After the corn was harvested and the stalks dried out, trails were plowed through the field. Lurking in its shadows were Freddy Kruger, Michael Myers of horror movie fame, and an assortment of generic ghouls and goblins, ready to jump out and scare the brave souls that dared enter.

"I was worried we might not have large crowds after what happened to Hazel," I said. When Hazel Martin was murdered earlier in the season, the business owners worried it would scare tourists off.

Ethan nodded, his blond hair falling across his forehead. He pushed it back. "It is a pretty wonderful sight. Hazel Martin's murder didn't run off the tourists after all."

Pumpkin Hollow was a small town that boasted a Halloween theme year-round. But the Halloween season was from Labor Day to mid-November and the town relied on this season to bring in revenue to keep it going.

"It's a huge relief," I said, pushing back my long hair. It was medium brown and I wondered if I should color it orange or green to celebrate the season.

"Are you going into the corn maze?" he asked. Ethan was a police officer but was off duty and wearing jeans and a black t-shirt. I had to tilt my head up to look him in the eye.

"Maybe," I said, looking at the entrance.

"You're not scared, are you? Because if you are scared, there's always the straw maze. I'm sure the kindergartners won't mind you joining them."

I narrowed my eyes at him. "Listen, smarty-pants, I'm not afraid of the corn maze. It's just kind of crowded in there right now."

He chuckled. "I haven't seen very many people go in there. It's pretty dark now and the ghouls will come out from the shadows. But don't be chicken. They don't bite that hard."

I sighed and crossed my arms over my chest, giving him the eye. It had been years since I had been in the corn maze. Ten years to be exact. October of my senior year of high school, I had gone through the corn maze with a group of friends that included a boyfriend who I had felt I was on the verge of breaking up with. The corn maze sealed the deal when he hid behind some corn stalks and jumped out at me, squirting fake blood on my face and blouse. Yeah. That did it for me. I went home with one of my friends and left him behind, refusing to answer his phone calls.

Ethan tilted his head and looked at me questioningly.

"Fine. Let's go through the corn maze," I said. What could go wrong? I knew most of the actors that played the scary creeps hiding in the maze. It wasn't like they would hurt me.

"I knew you'd do it," he said. "If you get too scared, you can hold my hand."

I snorted as we headed toward the entrance. "I don't think that will be necessary."

Ethan and I hadn't been friends in school. In fact, in the seventh grade he had started a rumor that I had spiders in my hair. Try living that one down in a Halloween town.

Ethan took out his wallet for the entrance fee and I stuck my hand in my pocket for the money I had stowed there so I wouldn't have to carry my purse around.

"I got it," he said over his shoulder as he handed the zombie at the entrance the money.

"Oh, you don't have to do that," I insisted. It felt a little awkward to have someone I really didn't know very well pay my entrance fee. I had been away from Pumpkin Hollow for ten years, earning three master's degrees at the University of Michigan, and had lost contact with most of the kids I knew in high school. After ten years of studying, I still didn't know what I wanted to do with my life and here I was, back in the small town I thought I had left behind for good.

"I said I got it," he said glancing over his shoulder.

"Thank you," I said. There was no use arguing with him when the police officer in him came out.

We could hear screams coming from the corn maze and if I was being truthful, I felt a little nervous about the whole thing. It was dumb. There was nothing to worry about, but having someone jump out at you with a chainsaw can be scary even if you know they won't actually hurt you.

As we walked down the first path, I heard a growl coming from the stalks of corn. I stepped a little closer to Ethan.

He chuckled. "I must have left my dog out. He won't hurt you, though."

I took a deep breath and smiled. It was all in fun. Right?

"What's that?" I asked, pointing at a hulking figure in the shadows up ahead.

"Let's go find out," he said with a grin.

There were dim lights put up in the corners of the maze, but large portions of the maze were in complete darkness. I kept my eye on the dark figure as we approached it.

"Hey buddy, you lost?" Ethan asked it.

The thing started groaning and swaying back and forth. It was covered in a black cloak and a blank black mask covered its face. I pressed against the walls of the corn maze, hoping it wouldn't reach out and grab me.

"Let's go."

The groans got louder. Ethan laughed again and stepped around it.

As I passed, it reached out and took hold of my wrist. I screamed, jerking my arm away from it. The figure dressed in black screamed along with me, and then broke out in loud cackles.

I broke into a trot and headed up the path. Ethan brought up the rear, still laughing.

"Don't talk to strangers, Mia. It's stranger danger 101," he called to me.

"Yeah, thanks for the advice, Ethan," I said, trying to control the fear. It was dumb to be scared of this place, but I couldn't help it. I stopped and let him catch up to me. "This was a bad idea."

"It will be fine," he said when he caught up. "I won't let them get you. This is what the Halloween season is all about."

"I prefer the family-friendly entertainment," I said. We walked on, turning a corner. A green goblin jumped out at me and I screamed again and ran, dodging him as I passed.

I heard footsteps running after me and I glanced over my shoulder. It was Ethan and he was still laughing. I slowed to a stop and turned toward him, hands on my hips.

"What's so funny? I don't see anything to laugh about," I huffed.

"Honestly, Mia, I didn't think this was going to be so entertaining." He bent over and put his hands on his thighs, still laughing and trying to catch his breath.

"I'm glad someone is enjoying themselves," I said and turned around and headed down the path. Two teenagers pushed past me, laughing and screaming, and ran up ahead.

"I'm sorry, Mia, you are correct. This is no laughing matter," Ethan said, trying to sound serious. He straightened up and caught up to me.

I smirked. "Whatever, Mr. Officer. Laugh all you want. I'm going to find a hole in the side of this maze to escape through and get out of here."

"You don't want to do that. You'll miss all the excitement. We haven't seen Freddy yet."

"I can do without seeing Freddy. I should have trusted my instincts and done the straw bale maze."

"The first rule of avoiding assault is to trust your instincts," he informed me. "You should have listened to yourself."

I snorted and we walked side by side down the path. The hair on the back of my neck stood on end as I squinted my eyes in the dark. There was a lot of screaming going on and I really did wonder if there was a way out of this thing without going all the way to the end. The path we were following dead-ended in the dark and we turned back.

"How do we get out of this thing?" I asked him.

"If you want your freedom, you've got to earn it," he said. "That's why they call it a maze. It will be amazing if you live through it."

"Ha ha," I said.

A mummy with bloody bandages jumped out at me and I screamed and ran again. I let Ethan catch up with me and we walked on while I searched for an exit. The air was humid inside the maze with the evening turning warmer than expected, and I wished I hadn't worn a light windbreaker. All the running I was doing was making me sweat.

We turned another corner and came face to face with a chainsaw-wielding madman with a white-painted and scarred face and red hair. He pulled the start pulley and revved the chainsaw at us. I screamed and ran down a path leading away from him.

My senses told me I was headed the opposite direction from the exit, but I didn't care. I was done with things jumping out at me and I was going to make my own exit in the side of the maze if need be.

"Mia, slow down!" I heard Ethan call.

It was fully dark now and there weren't any lights down this corridor. I kept running. At the last moment, I realized I was going to hit a wall. I tried to pull up, but hit the cornstalks, tripped over something on the ground, and sprawled onto the hard-packed path.

My head spun and I gasped for air. I tried to inhale, but my lungs didn't seem to work after the fall knocked the air out of them.

"Mia, are you okay?" Ethan asked, catching up and kneeling beside me. He was breathing hard and put one hand on my shoulder.

I looked up at him, still trying to get some air in. After what seemed like a very long moment, my breath caught and I inhaled. I willed myself not to cry with the effort of breathing.

"Mia, are you okay?" he asked again.

I nodded and forced myself to smile, pushing myself up onto my elbows. I rolled over and winced.

"My ankle hurts," I said, sitting up and trying to pull my leg closer so I could get a look at it.

"Be careful, it might be broken," Ethan said, and took his phone out of his pocket. He turned on the flashlight app and shined it onto my ankle. "Tell me if I'm hurting you."

I winced as he gently slid the cuff of my jeans up away from my ankle. "Ow," I said.

"Sorry," he said. "Lie down, it might make it easier. I know a little first aid, but we may need to call an ambulance if you can't walk out of here."

"Oh, no, don't do that," I said, and lay down on the ground. I could just imagine EMTs having to drag a gurney back through the maze to bring me out while everyone gathered around to watch.

"It's starting to swell a little," he said as he ran gentle fingers over my ankle.

I gasped. "Ow."

"Sorry. Sit up and let's see if you can put any weight on it," he said and put his hand out for me to take.

I took a deep breath and glanced to my left before sitting up again. That was when I screamed.

Chapter Two

Trying to get out of a corn maze with thirty other people screaming and running through it is no easy task. Trying to do it with a sprained ankle is nearly impossible.

Ethan called for backup and rounded up some of the organizers to clear out the maze. He had deposited me onto a nearby wagon and went back through the maze to make sure everyone was out.

Freddy Krueger sidled over to me and I looked up at him, not sure if I should scream or not. Running away was out of the question, so I hoped he wanted to be friends.

"Hey, Mia, it's me. John Jones," he said, pulling his mask off. "Do you know what happened back there?"

I stared at him a moment, then shook myself. I had gone to school with John and he was safe. "There's a body back there," I whispered.

He looked at me, eyebrows furrowed. "A real one?"

I nodded. "Yeah. Ethan thought it was a prop. It was laying among the corn stalks in a back corridor. But when he checked, it wasn't a prop."

"A real dead person?" he asked skeptically. "Because there's some pretty realistic looking props planted in there."

"Ethan's probably pretty good at being able to tell a real dead body from a prop," I said, trying not to sound sarcastic.

"Yeah, I guess so. Well, that's not good," he said, taking this in. "Did you see what happened to the dead guy? Was it a man?"

I nodded and breathed out. "A man. A dead man. I saw his face, but it all happened so fast and it was so dark, that I couldn't tell who it was." This was true, but Ethan got a good look at the man. I decided not to name names. When the victim's identity got out, it would spread like wild fire.

"That's crazy," he said, looking at the maze. "And scary."

We both turned toward the parking lot when four police cruisers pulled up, lights flashing and sirens blaring. An ambulance pulled up behind them.

Ethan walked out of the corn maze and went to the other officers. After a minute, he pointed at the corn maze. Three of the officers headed to different clusters of people and started talking to them. The rest of the officers went into the corn maze and Ethan made his way over to me.

"Hi, John. How are you doing, Mia?"

"I'm in one piece," John answered.

"I'm okay," I said. My mind felt a little disjointed and I kept asking myself if I had really seen a dead body among the corn stalks. How did he get back there? He had been almost completely off the path and was lying between the stalks that made up the exterior wall of the maze. Everything seemed surreal.

"How is your ankle?" he asked.

"I don't think it's as bad as I first thought. Help me down and I'll see if I can put weight on it," I said.

He put his arm around me and helped me slide down to the ground. I landed on my good foot and delicately put the other one down. My ankle screamed in pain when I put weight on it. I took a deep breath and waited. After a moment, the pain eased up and I found I could put the slightest bit of weight on my toes if I was careful.

"Careful," he said, as I leaned on him for support.

"It's not too bad," I said as he helped me walk a few steps.

"It's not too good, either," he said, and helped me back to the wagon. "I'm going to be tied up a while. Do you want to call your mom and have her pick you up?"

"Maybe in a bit. I'll stay a while."

He nodded. "I'm sure someone is going to need to question you," he said.

"Who was it back there?" John asked.

"I really can't say right now," Ethan said. "The other officers will have to interview you, too. In case you saw something while you were in there."

He shrugged. "No problem, but I was so busy scaring people that I didn't see much."

"It'll only take a few minutes of your time," Ethan said.

John nodded. "I'm going to go see if anyone saw anything. Let me know when they need to talk to me," he said and headed toward a small group of actors that worked in the maze.

When John was out of earshot, I turned to Ethan. "Is this really happening? It feels surreal."

He turned toward me. "I'm afraid so. The mayor, Stan Goodall, was murdered. That's between you and me. We have to keep it quiet until his family is notified and an announcement is made."

I nodded. The mayor was the last person I would have imagined would be lying dead in a corn maze. "Could you tell how he died? I looked away." I had seen blood on his arm and on the front of his shirt, but I didn't want to see any more.

He nodded. "From the wound in his chest and the blood on the front of his shirt, it looks like he was shot, but the medical examiner will have to determine that for sure. There was a lot of blood. I'd say he was shot several times."

I tried to process this. What had the mayor been doing in the maze? Had it happened while I was running from the chain-saw-wielding madman? I doubted anyone would have heard gunshots over the sound of the chainsaw. But it had only been a minute or two from the time I ran into the madman until I ran down the corridor and tripped. I supposed it was possible, but I doubted he would have died that fast.

"How awful," I said, shaking my head.

"I think he's been out there a while. His body was cold," he said.

"Oh, good," I said, nodding.

He raised an eyebrow at me. "Good?"

"No, I don't mean, good, he's dead. I mean I'm glad it didn't happen when we were in there."

"Me too. With everyone running around, someone else could have been shot along with the mayor," he said. "I think it probably happened before the maze opened this evening."

A car pulled up and parked alongside one of the police cars. The driver's side door swung open and I recognized Jerry Crownover, the mayor's brother-in-law.

"That was fast," I said.

"I guess any one of us could identify the mayor's body, but they probably wanted a family member just to keep everything official."

"Why would he come out here to identify the body? Seems kind of crude. And who would kill the mayor?" I asked, thinking out loud.

"I'm sure they don't want to move the body and disturb evidence. As for who would want to kill the mayor, it's too early to tell anything yet. But there's a lot of anger over the mayor calling a vote to end the Halloween season," Ethan said. "Maybe it had something to do with that."

I swallowed. The mayor and Jerry Crownover had called for a vote to end the Halloween season because Pumpkin Hollow was struggling financially. I hoped someone wasn't retaliating against the mayor, but Ethan was right. Emotions were running high over losing what was our town's heritage. This was the second murder in less than a month and two murders close together were not going to help draw tourists in. I didn't like this.

"I really hope someone didn't kill him over the Halloween season," I said softly.

"You wait right here," Ethan said and went to one of the other officers. They had begun stringing up crime scene tape around the corn maze. I wasn't sure how big the maze was, but I thought it might be as large as a third of an acre. That was going to take a lot of crime scene tape.

People hovered nearby, watching the police officers walk from person to person with notebooks in hand. I sighed. It was terrible that someone had murdered the mayor. His family would be devastated. But the town would suffer as well. How were we going to get past this? The town's reputation was sliding downhill fast.

"Hey, Mia," Jasper Smith said as he approached me. Jasper was Ethan's partner and was also off duty, dressed in jeans and a t-shirt.

"Hi, Jasper. Did they call you out on your day off?"

"No, I heard it over the scanner. I thought they could use some help," he said. "Were you in the maze?"

"Yes. Ethan and I found him," I said.

"Wow. Well, I guess you got your money's worth tonight," he said.

"More than I wanted, and a sprained ankle to boot," I said lifting my leg a little.

He smiled. "I'm so sorry. Do you want me to take you to the hospital?"

"No, I think it'll be fine. I can put a little weight on it. I just hope this doesn't hurt our efforts to bring business back to Pumpkin Hollow," I said, and then thought better of it. "I guess that isn't one of the most sensitive things to say. I feel bad about what happened and I feel bad for his family."

"I understand. Look on the bright side. This might make business better. People like the macabre, especially when we're supposed to be a family-oriented attraction. Rumors might bring more people in."

"I'd rather we get our tourists another way," I said.

"I agree," he said. "I'm going to see if they need my help."

I waited as the police finished taping things off and speaking to the people hanging around. It was almost midnight by the time Ethan was finished.

"I'll give you a ride home," he said, tiredly. "We can pick up your car tomorrow."

"Okay," I said and yawned. It was my right ankle that had been sprained and I wouldn't be driving for a while.

"How's the ankle?"

"Not too bad. It swelled a little, but it's not very bad."

He helped me hobble over to his car and opened the passenger car door. I sat down sideways on the seat, swung my legs into the car, and pulled the seat belt across my body.

"Sorry this wasn't as fun as it should have been," he said when he got into the driver's seat.

"Me too. Especially for the mayor and his family."

I sighed and closed my eyes, laying my head on the seat's headrest. This was not what I had in mind when I thought about helping put the town back on the map.

Chapter Three

I was on crutches the next day when I went to work. Thankfully it was a Monday, so I didn't have to wear a costume. Pumpkin Hollow business owners usually dressed up in costumes on the weekends during the Halloween season. I couldn't imagine trying to get pantyhose over my wrapped ankle or wearing the cute little black boots that went along with my Little Red Riding Hood costume. The sprain was pretty minor, but I wanted to keep my weight off it as much as possible with the crutches.

"What happened to you?" Andrea Stone asked when she came in for her afternoon shift.

I was sitting on a stool behind the counter with my ankle wrapped and the crutches leaning against the display case. Mom had hired Andrea and Lisa Anderson, a high school student, to help out part-time and they had been lifesavers. It felt good to be able to leave the shop in their capable hands from time to time and Mom didn't have to work as hard as she usually did.

"I had a little accident in the corn maze last night," I explained. "I tripped over something."

"Was John Jones chasing you? I heard he's really getting into his part as Freddy Krueger."

"No, I got scared by a chainsaw-wielding madman and ran like a fool through the dark and tripped. Unfortunately, I tripped over a body."

She gasped. "A real body? Not a prop?"

I nodded, and opened the bag of orange and black jellybeans I held. "I'm not sure if the family has been notified yet, so do me a favor and don't repeat this?"

"Of course I won't mention it," she said, leaning toward me. "Who was it?"

"It was the mayor," I whispered, popping an orange jellybean into my mouth.

Her face went pale.

"That's terrible," she said.

"Tell me about it. I don't know what's going on with this town. First Hazel Martin, now the mayor."

She reached into her purse and pulled out a small gift box. Her hand trembled a little as she held the box.

"I made you something," she said and handed me the box. "I made one for Lisa, your mom, and myself, too."

"That's sweet of you," I said in surprise and took the box from her. I opened the small cardboard gift box and inside was a cute jack-o-lantern pin resting on a layer of cotton. The face was made of tiny orange beads and it had green rhinestone eyes, nose, and mouth. "This is darling, Andrea! I love it."

She beamed. "Thanks. My mom got some new beads in, and I had an idea and went with it." Andrea's black hair sported a red streak on one side and her blue eyes twinkled.

"It's really cute," I said and removed it from the box and pinned it to my top.

"Thanks," she said and her hand went to the collar on her own blouse.

"Where's your pin?" I asked her.

She smiled. "I must have left it on my dresser."

"We'll all have to wear them when we work. I think it would be cute for us all to wear matching pins."

"We should totally do that," she said and climbed onto the other stool.

"I love the pin," I repeated. It was thoughtful of her to think of all of us.

She was quiet a few moments, and then said, "I guess the mayor's murder might kind of help the town, don't you think?"

"What do you mean?" I asked, looking at her.

She clasped her hands together in her lap, crossed her legs, and shrugged. "The mayor wanted to get rid of the Halloween season. Now that he's dead, we don't have to worry about that. It sounds like a stroke of good luck to me."

I was a little stunned by her words. "I'm sure his death had nothing to do with the Halloween season. I doubt it would help the season, anyway. Someone will take his place and they might want to end the Halloween season, too."

"I doubt it. The mayor was a selfish jerk. He didn't care one bit about this town or the people that live here. I bet we get someone new that wants things to stay the way they are," she said, sounding sure of herself.

"I suppose that might happen," I said. "I think it might be premature to talk about it at this point." It bothered me that she was jumping to conclusions about the mayor's death. Ethan had brought it up the night before, but I couldn't imagine someone killing the mayor over the upcoming vote on the Halloween season.

I took a deep breath. But what if it was true? Pumpkin Hollow had been a Halloween-themed town since shortly after World War Two. When soldiers came back after the war, they needed employment and someone had come up with the idea. It stuck. My grandparents had opened the Pumpkin Hollow Candy Store about that time, and later handed it down to my parents.

The bell over the door jingled and I looked up to see Ethan walk through it.

"Hey Mia, Andrea," he said, nodding in her direction.

"Hi Ethan," I said.

"How's your ankle?" he asked.

"Not too bad. Just a slight sprain, but I brought crutches along to keep my weight off of it."

"That's a good idea. I'm glad it wasn't worse."

"Have you heard anything new?" I asked.

He shook his head. "Not really. The investigation is just getting started," he said. He was dressed in his police uniform and looked dashing. Not that I noticed things like that.

"I think someone killed the mayor because of the Halloween season," Andrea said to him. "It seems obvious. Don't you think so?"

Ethan turned toward her. "I really don't think it's obvious, but I suppose it's a possibility. We won't know anything until the investigation is finished."

Andrea pressed her lips together and looked down at her hands. Then she looked up at Ethan. "He was a real jerk when I had him as a teacher in school. I don't know how he ever got to be mayor."

I looked at her. "Did you have him for glee club or math?" Most schools would have had a music teacher head up the glee club, but the high school had been struggling financially and most of the music programs had been cut. When the chorus teacher had retired, Stan Goodall was pressed into service to take the helm of the struggling glee club.

She nodded. "He hated being the teacher for glee club. He said they forced it on him and he didn't care if we made it to competitions or not."

"That's a shame. He shouldn't have taken his frustrations out on the kids," I said.

"The real shame was that we did a fundraiser and he said we didn't sell enough candy to go to regionals. But we each knew how much money we made from our sales and we did sell enough to make our goal. I could have had a music scholarship if we had gone to regionals. Then I wouldn't be stuck attending the junior college."

"I've heard rumors of the fundraiser money disappearing," I said. "You're right. That's a real shame."

She sighed and looked at her hands in her lap. "Is your mom in the back?" she asked, slipping down off the stool.

"Yes, she's making pumpkin truffles."

"I'll see if she needs help," she said, and took another small box out of her purse before heading to the kitchen in the back room.

"It seems Andrea isn't going to miss our illustrious mayor," Ethan said, leaning against the front counter.

"I hate to say it, but it might make things easier for us to keep the Halloween season alive. Not that I would kill anyone to make that happen, you understand," I said.

He chuckled. "I don't know. It seems like you have a lot invested in keeping the Halloween season alive."

I sobered. "I feel really bad about him being killed. I didn't like him, but he had a family that loved him," I said, slipping down off the stool and hopping over to the front counter. I held out the open bag of orange and black jellybeans.

"Thanks," he said, pulling out a few beans and popping them into his mouth. "Everyone's kind of shook up about it. The medical examiner says he was dead for at least twelve to twenty-four hours by the time we found him."

"Wow. No one missed him? No one else went into that part of the maze?"

"There aren't any lights back there because they decided not to put any actors back there. They figured the lack of lighting would keep people from wandering around. And if Stan was killed closer to twelve hours earlier and not twenty-four, his wife may have thought he was still at work."

"I guess the killer didn't count on a freaked-out candy merchant running away from a killer character and discovering the body," I said, popping another orange jellybean into my mouth.

"Nope. I have to wonder what the mayor was doing back there, though," he said.

"Is there another entrance or exit besides the obvious ones?"

He shook his head. "No, just those two. But they don't lock it up during the day or after hours. There's nothing in there after the actors leave, so no need to lock up anything."

I sighed. "I'd like to know what he was doing back there, too."

"That, my dear, is a mystery at this point," he said with a grin.

I sighed. Stan Goodall had been married to the former Miss Susan Crownover, the high school librarian. She didn't look like your typical librarian with her low-cut blouses and short skirts. The girls in school had gossiped about her, insisting she was dating some of the married male teachers on the sly. I had always thought it was a rumor until one day I caught her with one of them. I never told anyone.

"Was he married to Miss Crownover when we were still in school? I can't remember," I said.

"They got married after we graduated," he said. "When we were seniors there was a rumor Mr. Gonzales was seeing her, but he was married."

I looked at him. "It may have been true. I walked in on her and Mr. Gonzales in the library one day. They looked like they had been kissing and had just pulled away when I opened the door."

He shrugged. "You never know about rumors, do you?"

I shook my head. "I'm guessing she's been told he's dead?"

"Yeah, I went by last night."

"What?" I gasped. "You were off duty and it was late."

"I know, but the other officers were still processing the scene. After I dropped you off, I went back by the haunted farmhouse. Jerry Crownover said he needed to tell his sister, so I volunteered to go with him."

"I'm sorry you had to do that," I said. "That must have been awful."

He nodded, his lips making a thin line. "That's one thing I truly hate about this job. I'm glad I live in a small town. I've only had to do it one other time."

"I can't imagine," I said and handed him the bag of jelly beans again. Food always made me feel a little better and he needed it right then.

He smiled and reached into the bag. "How's the website for the town and the Halloween season going?"

"It's live now. I was going to show it off at the next city council meeting when we vote on whether to stop having the Halloween season, but—" and I stopped.

"What?" he asked.

"Maybe someone really did kill the mayor to keep him from ending the Halloween season. We were going to have a vote. Maybe he was killed before the vote could be taken."

"I suppose it's possible. But it seems like we could just vote and not kill people, you know? I mean, yes, the Halloween season is important, but important enough to kill someone over?"

"I don't know," I said. "I hope that wasn't it."

"Can I see the website?"

"Yes, of course," I said. I reached beneath the counter for the tablet I had stowed there and pulled it out. I brought up the website and showed it to him.

I had built the website as a way to draw in more tourists. The town's business had deteriorated while I was away at college. We desperately needed to prove the town could still be a viable source of income during the Halloween season. I was proud of what I had done and I was sure it was going to help. But now I was worried we would lose all that precious new business because of another murder.

"That looks great," Ethan said, tapping on a link. "Very nice. I like the maps of the town and the business listings. It's very professional looking." He looked up at me and smiled.

I felt a warmth go through my body when he smiled at me and I returned his smile. I couldn't help it. There was just something about him.

Chapter Four

"**M**illie, you need to keep exercising or your joints will fall apart," I warned the little dog. Millie was walking and I was hobbling with a cane around the Pumpkin Center Park. The little schnauzer-Chihuahua mix had her tail jauntily sticking straight up in the air. Millie was gray with black hair at the edges of her muzzle and feet. I had known Millie since she was a puppy. She was a senior citizen in dog years now and I had inherited her from a neighbor under dubious circumstances.

It was mid-morning and the candy store had been slow, so I decided both Millie and I could use some exercise. Mom said she didn't mind me leaving her alone, so I took the opportunity.

When I saw a police car pull up to the curb, I waved. Ethan got out of the cruiser and headed in my direction.

"Hi Ethan, what are you up to?" I asked, leaning on my cane. After a day of trying to get around on the crutches, I had swapped them for the cane.

"I'm heading to the mayor's house to speak to his wife, but I saw you and Millie and made a detour." He bent down and scratched Millie's ears. Millie looked up at him, closing her eyes in a blissful smile, and sat on her haunches.

"Well, she certainly appreciates that," I said. "Why are you going to speak to the mayor's wife?"

"She was pretty broken up the other night, so I didn't interview her. I need to know if someone may have been hanging around or if the mayor mentioned anything that might be suspicious," he said, straightening up.

I nodded. "Where's Jasper?" I was used to seeing the two of them together and it was odd he wasn't with Ethan.

"We had a couple of officers transfer out of the department, so we'll be on our own for a while. It's not like we have so much crime around here that we can't handle a few shifts alone," he said with a grin.

I tilted my head. "We didn't used to have much crime, you mean."

"It's just a fluke. Everything will return to normal. You'll see," he said, sounding confident. "I guess I better get going."

I nodded. But two murders in less than a month seemed like more than a fluke. "Ethan, is there any chance I can go with you to talk to Mayor Goodall's wife, Susan?" I asked. "You know, just as a ride-along. That's what they call it on TV, isn't it?"

He studied me a moment. "And why would you want to ride along?"

I shrugged. "I don't know. I guess you could say I have a stake in this town. I was, after all, made a liaison, howbeit unofficially, to all things Halloween. I'd be interested to hear if she thought someone had a murder-worthy grudge against the mayor and whether it had anything to do with the Halloween season. I know it isn't really any of my business, of course."

He considered it a moment. "I suppose it wouldn't hurt. Technically we should get approval first, but it should be okay," he said. "We just won't mention it to anyone."

I smiled. "Mum's the word. Let's drop Millie off at my house on the way over."

I WAS GLAD ETHAN LET me ride along; I just hoped he didn't get into trouble for it. We took Millie back to my house and then drove over to the mayor's house. Ethan parked the police car in front of the mayor's house.

The house was a beige stucco ranch style and boring. I was a little surprised by how small it was, but then I remembered the mayor's position didn't pay much more than a teacher's salary. His income probably hadn't changed when he went from schoolteacher to mayor.

I left my cane in the car and did my best to limp as little as possible as we walked up to the door. Ethan rang the doorbell and the door swung open almost immediately.

"Officer Banks," Mrs. Goodall said. Then she looked at me. "I don't believe we've met."

"I'm Mia Jordan," I said, and shook her hand that she offered. "You probably don't remember me from high school."

She smiled at me. "You do look very familiar," she said, studying my face. "Sorry. I can't quite place you."

"It's been a while," I said, smiling. I was glad she didn't remember me. The unfortunate incident where I interrupted her and Mr. Gonzales in the library, was probably better forgotten.

"Mia is a liaison to the town," Ethan explained. "Mrs. Goodall, I need to ask you some questions. I hope you don't mind."

"Of course not," she said. "Come in."

We followed her into the formal living room and took the loveseat she motioned toward. I couldn't help but notice she looked the same as she had when I was in high school. Her blond hair was bleached almost white and it was still long and put up in a messy bun like she wore it when I was in school.

There didn't appear to be one wrinkle on her face. I thought she must have had really good genes or a really good skin cream.

"Mrs. Goodall, I'm terribly sorry for your loss," I said, crossing my legs. I remembered my wrapped ankle that bulged beneath my pant leg and uncrossed my legs.

She smiled, but it looked strained. "Thank you. I'm afraid I'm still in shock. I just never expected something like this." She clasped her hands in her lap and looked at them.

"That's understandable," Ethan said. "Mrs. Goodall, did you notice anything different in the last couple of weeks? Did your husband mention anything that might be of interest?"

She looked up and shook her head, her eyes now shiny with tears. "I just can't believe it. He went to the office every morning like he always did. He never mentioned anything out of the ordinary."

Ethan began writing in his notebook. "Was there anyone suspicious hanging around the house?" he asked, and then looked up at her.

"No. I never noticed anything at all," she said. "We had a very good marriage."

I blinked. Ethan hadn't asked about her marriage. "How long were you married?" I asked.

"Seven years," she said. "We were both married before, but it didn't work out for either of us. My ex was a body-builder with a roving eye and I got rid of him in a hurry. But when Stan and I got together, it was like magic. Everything seemed to work for us. I just don't understand who would want to kill him." She reached over to pull a tissue out of the box on the coffee table and dabbed at her eyes.

"He never mentioned anything that seemed out of the ordinary?" Ethan asked. "No person of interest that might have been causing him trouble?"

She shook her head. "Nothing. He went to work that morning and didn't come back. I loved him so much. It was like this was the marriage I had been waiting for all my life. And he was so happy. He told me all the time how happy he was. Everyone always commented on how happy we looked."

I felt bad for her. I couldn't imagine being woken up in the middle of the night and being told your husband was never coming home. If she really was as happy as she said she was, it was a real tragedy.

"Stan was well liked by everyone," she said, and beamed. "The kids at the high school loved him and were so sad when he left. But he had bigger career plans. He had wanted to be mayor since he was a boy."

"Really?" I asked. "That's great that he got to realize a childhood dream." I wondered about the rumors about missing fundraiser money while he was at the high school, but I wasn't going to bring it up.

She nodded. "The kids gave him a plaque when he left the school. Let me get it." She jumped up from the sofa and disappeared down a hallway.

I turned to Ethan and he shrugged.

"I thought he left because of missing funds?" I whispered, leaning close to him.

She was back before he could answer and I sat up straight.

"Here it is. He kept in on the wall of his office," she said and handed it to me.

Ethan leaned over to look at it with me. The plaque was a thank-you for Stan Goodall's service from the school district. Nowhere did it say it was from any student or student group.

I looked up at her and handed the plaque back to her. "How awesome is that? I can see where he would want to keep it on the wall so he could be reminded of the school's appreciation."

She gazed at the plaque and smiled. "He was so proud of this. Not one day goes by where someone at the school doesn't stop by the library and tell me how wonderful he was and how much they miss him."

"That's really wonderful," Ethan said.

I smiled back at her, but I had a hard time believing Stan Goodall was as well-loved as she said. I had no proof he had embezzled funds, but even if he hadn't, I didn't remember him being a popular teacher. I could remember kids groaning when they found out they had to take his math class. He had been less than helpful as a teacher, and Andrea had confirmed how little he was liked.

Ethan asked her a few more questions and we left. She stood on the front step and watched until we pulled away.

"Well? Did you find out anything you needed to know?" I asked when we were back in the car.

"Not really. They had a happy marriage and there wasn't anything different about their lives before her husband was murdered. And her husband was an awesome teacher."

"I don't remember him being an awesome teacher," I said.

"Me either," he agreed.

"Did you think she would say her marriage wasn't a happy marriage?" I asked. I wasn't sure how much Ethan knew and whether he had to keep some of it from me.

"Not really, but you never know what someone might say that gives something away."

"It seemed like she was really trying to press the point that she had a happy marriage. It was odd."

"I noticed that, too. But maybe she's been going over all the good things about their marriage in her mind and that's made her sad for what she's going to miss now that he's gone," he said.

"You're a positive thinker, aren't you?" I said with a grin.

He shrugged and smiled. "I don't want to jump to conclusions, but I've made a mental note of her happy marriage. She was really, really happy in her marriage."

"It's just a sad situation," I said. "I hope his killer is arrested soon. I guess there isn't much that can be done about the news reporting on this. I hope it doesn't hurt the season."

"Me too," he said and turned a corner.

"Wait. Did that sound selfish? It did, didn't it?" I asked, thinking it over. "I mean, the most important thing is finding Stan Goodall's killer. The Halloween season will be what it will be."

"It's not selfish. There are a lot of families that depend on the tourists coming to town and spending money. Even though there's been a murder, we still need to make sure the tourists are happy."

I nodded. There were a lot of livelihoods hanging in the balance. Murder or no murder, we needed to concentrate on that.

Chapter Five

I was in the kitchen making peanut butter fudge when I heard the sirens. I put down the pan of fudge I had in my hands and pulled my apron off. I tossed the apron onto a counter and headed to the front of the store.

"What's going on?" I asked as two fire trucks with sirens blaring drove past the front of the candy store.

"I don't know. Two police cars just went by, too," Mom said as she stood by the front window watching the fire trucks drive by.

I hurried to the front door. A smaller fire truck sped down the street. Off in the distance, I could see angry black funnels of smoke reaching toward the sky. "Oh, my gosh. Is that the haunted farmhouse?"

"I can't tell from here," Mom said. "It's in that direction, though."

"I'm going to take a look," I said, and went to get my purse and keys.

AS I DROVE TOWARD THE haunted farmhouse, the black plumes of smoke grew larger. Other people had the same idea I had and there was a trail of cars heading in the same direction. There's not a lot to do in a small town, and although I don't normally chase fire trucks, I was doing it today.

When I got close, I could see that the corn maze and straw bale maze were on fire. I pulled off the road where I wouldn't be a nuisance to the emergency workers and parked. I walked toward the farmhouse, praying it hadn't caught fire as well. My ankle was nearly healed at this point and I was glad. Walking on the uneven shoulder of the road would have been difficult with a sprained ankle.

"I wonder what happened?" Amanda asked as she caught up with me. Amanda was my best friend from high school and, along with her fiancé Brian, ran the Little Coffee Shop of Horrors. She had parked her car behind mine, having heard the sirens as well.

"I don't know. I hope they can save the farmhouse," I said, looking at her. "This is terrible." The smell of smoke hung thick in the air and I coughed. It probably wasn't a great idea to get this close to the fire, but I couldn't help myself. The mazes were an important part of the Halloween season and we were losing them.

We got closer and stood in the parking lot and watched the mazes burn. My eyes teared up and I wasn't sure if it was from the smoke or the fact that the fire was sweeping across the mazes at a dizzying pace. The firemen were working at putting the fire out, with hoses pumping water forcefully onto the fire. The corn maze was dry and the fire was consuming it at a dizzying pace, but the firemen worked relentlessly at putting it out.

"So much for the Halloween season," Amanda said, leaning against a black Jeep.

I looked at her again, but didn't say anything. The farmhouse was a big draw with its mazes, pumpkin field, and hay rides. The Halloween season was taking a big hit.

I saw Ethan with some of the other police officers near the farmhouse. The door was open and two of them were going in and out. Thankfully no one lived in the farmhouse. It was just for looks with its broken windows and peeling paint. At night, ghostly apparitions danced in front of the windows via a light machine on a timer. Ethan turned on a garden hose and began spraying the grass around the house. I went to him.

"Hey," I said, walking up behind him.

"Hey," he said, glancing at me. There was soot smudged on his nose. "This might not make much of a difference, but I felt like I needed to do something."

"It looks like they're getting the fire out pretty fast," I said. And they were. The straw maze was smoldering now and there were only a few orange flames still eating up the cornstalks. Smoke curled up to the sky from the blackened ground, but the fire had retreated quickly.

"Yeah, thankfully none of the structures caught on fire," he said. "This is a mess for the Halloween season."

"I know. I can't believe this is happening. Wait. Where are the horses?" I said, looking toward the barn. "Are they still in there? What if the fire spreads?"

"They're out in the field. The caretaker puts them in the far pasture to graze every morning. He and a couple of other people are out there, standing at the ready to move the horses in case the fire spreads."

"Oh, good," I said, turning back to the mazes. "This is bad. Who reported the fire?"

"The caretaker. After he turned the horses out this morning, he went to pick up grain at the feed store. When he got back, the fire was going. He called 911 and then headed over to watch the horses," he said, turning the hose on the outside of the house.

I wrapped my arms around myself. The Halloween season had started out badly and was only getting worse. What would we do without attractions to draw in tourists? Some of the businesses would survive if there were no Halloween season, but many would close.

I sighed. Ethan glanced at me, and then went to shut off the hose.

"They did a great job getting that fire out," he said. "Everything's so dry here. If the caretaker hadn't gotten back when he did, the whole place would have been gone in a matter of minutes."

"Who owns this place?" I asked him.

He shrugged. "I don't really know. When we were in high school, the Davises owned it, but when the older generation passed away, I think their grandchildren sold it to someone from out of town."

"That's a shame it isn't owned by someone local," I said. Someone that didn't live here wouldn't understand how special the Halloween season was the way a local would. The farmhouse was important. But then, whoever owned it had kept it running without living here, so maybe they had some idea.

"It really is a shame," he agreed, dropping the end of the hose on the ground. "I'm going to talk to the fire captain. Try and stay out of trouble." He gave me a wicked grin. I narrowed my eyes at him and watched him go.

I surveyed the damage. I wasn't sure how much the city got from taxes on the income the farmhouse brought in, but this was going to leave a hole in the tax budget. How many people wouldn't even bother to stop by when they heard there were no mazes? The corn maze had been a popular attraction.

I coughed and wiped the tears running down my cheeks. I wasn't crying; the smoke was just irritating my eyes. The ground where the mazes had stood was still smoldering and the smoke burned my throat.

And then I wondered if the police had found all the evidence they needed to find the mayor's killer. The maze had remained closed since the mayor's body was found, but I thought it must have been difficult to search for evidence. I sighed. Now there was nothing but a burned-out field to search.

There was something rotten in Pumpkin Hollow.

Chapter Six

While the fire department finished putting out the smoldering mazes, I made a quick trip to the local gas station. I had an ice chest in the trunk of my car and I filled it up with ice and sodas before heading back to the farmhouse.

When I pulled up to the farmhouse, I got out and waved to Ethan.

"The good news is, the fire's out," he said when he got to me. "The bad news is, the mazes are a complete loss."

I shook my head. "I figured as much," I said sadly. "I brought drinks for everyone. I figured they could use them."

"Thanks. I'm sure they'll be appreciated," Ethan said, and picked up the ice chest for me. He carried it to where the corn maze had stood and set it down on the ground next to the burned area. He opened the lid for the firemen.

"I hate to see it this way," I said, looking over the still smoking ground. "I guess we could have some more straw bales trucked in and rebuild it, but the corn maze was what really drew people in."

"That's a possibility," he said, looking over the burned field. "The corn and straw were so dry, they didn't stand a chance."

I sighed. "I'm at a loss as to what to do."

"Soda?" he asked me.

I nodded and pulled a ginger ale out of the ice chest. "No one saw anyone leaving the place? With it being as dry as it is, you'd think they couldn't have gotten far before the whole thing went up in flames."

"I haven't heard that anyone saw anything, but we'll interview people," he said.

There was a crowd gathering near the farmhouse and I wondered if the firebug was still around, watching what they had done. Firebugs enjoyed watching their work. I clenched my teeth together and scanned the crowd for anyone looking suspicious.

Two of the firemen approached. I had gone to school with Josh Bilby and I recognized the older one as Calvin Stevens, an all-around nice guy that was involved with a lot of charitable functions in town.

"Just what I needed," Josh said, reaching into the ice chest for a soda.

"Mia Jordan to the rescue," Ethan said.

"Thanks, Mia," Calvin said, getting himself a soda.

"You're welcome. I'm just glad you guys got the fire put out as fast as you did."

Calvin nodded. "The good thing about a fire like this is that everything is exposed and we can get the water right on it."

"One positive, I guess," I said and took a sip of my soda. "At least the farmhouse didn't burn."

"A very big positive," Josh agreed.

"Does it look suspicious?" Ethan asked. "Could it have been something besides arson?"

"Someone could have tossed a cigarette out without thinking. If I had to guess though, I think there may have been an accelerant used, but we won't know for sure until samples are sent to the lab. Not that an accelerant was even necessary. Everything was so dry it would have gone up pretty quickly on its own. "

"Really," I said, thinking. "Do you mean something like gasoline?"

Calvin nodded. "That's the easiest thing for people to get a hold of. But it could have been lighter fluid, or any number of flammable liquids. Of course, they'll want to look into it more carefully before announcing something like that. And we need to keep that between ourselves."

"Of course," I said. I glanced at Ethan. He was looking at the corn maze, deep in thought. "Does the caretaker smoke? Or anyone else that works here?"

"I don't know, but we'll find out," Calvin said.

"Not much is going right for this town," Ethan said quietly, still looking at the burned mazes.

"I hope they find whoever did this," I said to Calvin. To me everything looked like a burned mess and I couldn't imagine knowing how to go about figuring out what happened. But a professional would know what they were looking for and maybe they would sort it out quickly.

"We have a good fire marshal," Josh said. "He'll figure it out."

"Let's hope whoever did this left something behind. It seems like everyone's against the Halloween season," I said. I heard my own voice crack and I silently cursed myself. I didn't want to cry over this, but I was afraid this might be a sign of things to come.

Ethan turned toward me. "Don't worry. We've got some great people that will be looking into this. They'll figure it out."

I nodded and took a sip of my ginger ale to clear the lump in my throat. The smell of smoke hung in the air and my eyes watered again.

"Did they get all the evidence from the mayor's murder?" I asked.

"I heard they wanted to do one more sweep of the corn maze, but I don't know if they ever got it done," he said. "I hope they did."

"Could be your murderer and our firebug are one and the same," Calvin said.

"It wouldn't surprise me a bit," Ethan said, looking out at the corn maze again. "If evidence is burned up, it can't be used against them."

I looked up at the blue sky, stretching my neck. I hadn't counted on murders and arson getting in the way of keeping the Halloween season alive. I sighed.

"We'll figure it out," Josh assured me again.

Two more firemen walked up and eyed the ice chest.

"Help yourself," I said, pasting a smile on my face. I would have to trust that these men knew what they were doing when looking for both a murderer and an arsonist. I had no other choice.

Amanda sidled up to me. "Hey," she said.

I turned to her. "Hey."

"People are saying it's the people against the Halloween season that set the fire," she whispered, and nodded toward the crowd that had gathered.

"Let them. There isn't anything we can do to stop them," I said, and took another drink of my soda. I bit back the bitterness I felt on the inside. We were doing all we could to save the season and I wasn't going to just roll over and let some jerk take it from us.

"I know. I just hate hearing them talk about how much trouble the Halloween season is bringing to the town. Then Jack

Malone said the murders wouldn't have happened if it weren't for the Halloween season. Other people agreed with him."

"Is that what they're saying?" I asked. "Why would they jump to that conclusion?"

She shrugged. "I don't know. I think certain people are spreading rumors and they're going to use the murders, and now the fire, to their advantage."

I shook my head. "Then we just won't let them. We'll figure something out."

"Let's take a walk," Ethan said to me.

I nodded and we walked along the edge of the corn maze, keeping our eyes on the ground.

"What are we looking for?" I asked him.

"Anything unusual," he said. "It might look hopeless, but the thing is, most criminals leave clues behind. They over-think everything and that makes them do foolish things that give them away."

"Like try to think like the police would think, but get it wrong?"

He nodded. "They get paranoid, thinking we'll think one thing when we're really thinking something else. Then they try and cover up the crime in such a way that it gives them away. Sure, we have to work at solving it, but in the end it seems like they always mess up and leave something obvious behind."

"That makes sense," I said. "Maybe I should watch more crime shows. That might help me understand more about how to catch a criminal."

He chuckled. "Because television is all about the facts?"

I smiled. "Okay, maybe that's a dumb idea. But I can see what you're saying about the criminals trying to outthink you and making mistakes because of it."

"Yup. You've just got to think like a paranoid criminal."

"I don't know if I can do that. The only crime I ever committed was in the second grade when I accidently borrowed Sally Mayfield's Barbie. I forgot to ask permission and stuffed it into my backpack, thinking no one would look. Unfortunately, my mother went through my backpack, looking for my lunch bag."

"You little thief," he said with a chuckle.

"In my defense, I'd like to point out that Sally was not supposed to bring toys to school. If Sally hadn't brought it, I wouldn't have taken it. Therefore, it was all Sally's fault."

"Criminals always want to blame their crimes on someone else. You've got the makings of a great criminal," he pointed out as we walked along the edge of the corn maze.

"Great. I just gave myself away to a cop," I said and laughed.

Chapter Seven

E than and I took a tour of the perimeters of both mazes, kicking at the dirt and turning over clumps of corn and straw. We found an old empty key ring but nothing of interest.

"That was a waste of time," I said as we walked up to the now almost empty ice chest. I put my empty ginger ale can next to the ice chest and looked at the remaining crowd.

"Have patience, Grasshopper," Ethan said with a smirk.

"Grasshopper," I muttered, still looking at the crowd. "I wonder if one of them is our arsonist. We should take them down to the police station and interrogate them."

Ethan chuckled. "We can shine a bright light in their eyes and shout at them until they confess," he said and put his soda can next to mine. "Let's go mingle. Act natural."

I smiled at him and headed for the crowd of people.

Fagan Branigan leaned against the barn and George Givens stood nearby.

"Hey, guys," I said.

"Hey, Mia. This has got to be about the worst thing that could happen to us," Fagan said.

"It sure isn't helpful," I agreed. "Did you see anything?"

Fagan owned the costume shop and was a big supporter of the Halloween season. Unfortunately, he was also in favor of getting rid of the mayor. If the fire had been started to hide murder evidence, Fagan might be a prime suspect.

He shrugged. "I was at work and heard the sirens. I came out to see what was happening." He shook his head. "This is really bad for the Halloween season."

"I agree," I said, nodding.

"They need to be interviewing everyone that stood up against the Halloween season at the last city council meeting," George said, looking at the burned-out corn maze. George Givens owned the gift shop. I had never heard him say anything bad about the mayor, but you never knew what someone did in private.

"I'm sure they'll be interviewing lots of people," I said. "Neither the killer nor the arsonist will get away with this." I sounded confident, but the truth was, I only hoped they caught the perpetrators. If evidence from the murder was burned up, things didn't look good.

I glanced over my shoulder at Ethan. He had moved over to another group of people and was talking to them.

"I'll tell you what's terrible," Jerry Crownover said, stepping up to where Fagan and I were standing. "What's terrible is an innocent man being shot and killed in cold blood. An innocent man who was serving his community. Not this!" he said motioning to the burned, empty fields.

"Serving his community?" Fagan said, standing up straight. "That idiot was the laziest person to be elected mayor in the history of Pumpkin Hollow."

I sucked in air. Fagan had a temper and he was not going to grieve the mayor's passing.

"How dare you!" Jerry exclaimed. "Stan Goodall was a great man. He deserves respect. He didn't deserve to be murdered in cold blood!"

Fagan laughed a deep, hearty laugh that had everyone looking at him. "You just don't understand who you're talking about," he said, putting his hands on his waist. "Everyone knows

Stan was a thief. Or are you forgetting about when he was fired from the high school because the fundraiser he was overseeing was suddenly missing funds?"

I looked at Ethan, begging him with my eyes to stop these two before something bad happened.

"I'll have you know Stan retired from the school district with honor. He got his full pension. If he had done something wrong, they wouldn't have given him his pension. People like you just love to gossip, don't you? You're a liar," Jerry said, taking three steps toward Fagan. Fagan stepped toward Jerry, towering over him as they stood toe to toe.

"Let's settle down here," Ethan said, coming to stand beside me.

"I'm tired of these liars, spreading trash about Stan," Jerry said. "When are you going to find Stan's killer? Maybe you should be taking a close look at people like this." Jerry nodded at Fagan.

"Why don't we all calm down here?" Ethan said. "We're working on finding the mayor's killer. We'll find whoever it is."

"Smokescreen. That's all your words are," Fagan said slowly. "The mayor was a crook and whoever killed him did this town a favor."

"I'm going to ask the two of you to disperse," Ethan said. "We're doing all we can to solve the murder and we don't need the two of you causing trouble."

"I'm not causing trouble," Jerry said. His face had turned red and sweat broke out on his forehead. "All I want is for justice to be done."

Fagan laughed again. "Justice. Justice was getting rid of that thief that called himself our mayor."

Another police officer walked up. "Why don't we all clear out? If you don't have anything constructive to say about the fire, then it's time to go."

Fagan snorted. "I have something constructive to say, but you probably don't want to hear it."

"You need to leave," Ethan said, stepping up close to Fagan. "Unless you would like to take a trip downtown?"

Fagan narrowed his eyes at Ethan for a moment, and then he smiled. "Sorry, Ethan. No problem here. I've got work to do back at the shop, anyway."

Ethan nodded. "Good. That's what I want to hear. Go back to your shop."

"That I'll do," Fagan said, and turned and headed for his car without looking back.

I gave Ethan a look, but didn't say anything. I knew Fagan felt strongly about the mayor and the Halloween season, but I didn't think he would do anything as drastic as commit murder. But maybe I was wrong.

"Now, what we need to know is if anyone saw anything regarding the fire," Ethan said to the remaining people standing around. "We can talk privately if you'd like."

"Was it arson?" Nelda Stevens asked. "It seems like we're having an awful lot of crime around here."

"We don't know at this point. We'd just like to know if anyone saw anything at all," Ethan told her.

People shook their heads or walked off, but no one stepped up to say they had seen anything. Jasper walked up and stood beside Ethan.

"What are you doing to solve Stan's murder?" Jerry asked crossing his arms over his chest.

"You really need to talk to the officer in charge of the investigation," Jasper said. "We're doing everything possible to find the killer."

Jerry sighed tiredly and looked at Jasper. "He was a good man. His family loved him."

"I understand that, Jerry," Jasper said. "But right now, we're working on the fire."

Jerry nodded and turned and headed to his car without another word.

I watched him go, feeling bad for him. I didn't blame him for feeling frustrated about the investigation.

Amanda stood up from her place on the front steps of the haunted farmhouse. "Mia, I've got to get back to work," she said. "Brian will be wondering why I haven't come back."

"I better get back, too. Mom will worry I got in an accident or burned up with the mazes," I said. I glanced at Ethan.

"I'll talk to you later," he said. "I'll bring your ice chest back to you."

I nodded and walked back to my car with Amanda.

"That was crazy back there," Amanda said.

"You can say that again," I agreed. "I hate that all of this is happening. Pumpkin Hollow has changed since I've been away."

"Honestly, Pumpkin Hollow has been the same little town it always has been up until recently," Amanda said as we walked.

"I don't understand why these things are happening. But we can't let this get us down. We've got to work on trying to figure out something else to draw the crowds in."

"I agree on that," I said and stopped in front of my car. "Amanda, how well do you know Fagan? I remember him from when I was young and my mom would take me to his shop to buy Halloween costumes, but I don't remember him having such a bad temper."

"Actually, he has always had something to say about everything. He's just one of those people that has their mouth going all the time, it seems. It doesn't help that it's louder than most other people's mouths."

"Do you think he could have lost his temper and killed the mayor?" I asked, then looked over my shoulder quickly to make sure I wasn't overheard.

"I don't know, Mia. Murder is such a big crime, you know? I can't imagine anyone doing that, but people do it all the time. Even though Fagan's got a big mouth, I still think he's a good guy. I'd hate to think he killed the mayor."

"I guess I shouldn't cast aspersions on anyone. At this point in time, anyone could have committed the murder."

"True," she agreed. "I better get back to the coffee shop. Brian's probably wondering what's keeping me."

"See you later," I said and she headed to her car.

I took one last look over my shoulder at the burned-out place where the mazes used to stand. I sighed. We needed to come up with another attraction, and fast.

Chapter Eight

"Thank you, and please come again," I said, as I handed change to my customer.

"Oh, I will. I love this town!" the woman said.

I smiled as she left. I loved repeat customers. I didn't know her by name, but I recognized her face. She didn't live in town, but she must live in one of the nearby cities.

"Well, in spite of the fire, it's still been a successful day," I said to my mother. She was putting chocolate peppermint truffles into the display case and I reached over and picked one up off the tray she carried. The inside was a deep dark chocolate flavored with peppermint and covered in a milk chocolate coating, then white chocolate that had been colored green was drizzled over the top.

"It has been, hasn't it? I think your website is helping," she said, closing up the display case.

"We've had over a thousand hits," I said, taking a bite of the truffle. I moaned. I could make the candy as well as my mother could, but for some reason it seemed more special when she made it. It was probably just a nostalgic thing for me.

"I'm so glad to hear it. And I'm glad you moved home, Mia. I missed you when you were away."

I smiled. "I missed you and Dad a lot. But I'm surprised how much I missed the town. I don't know why it surprises me, but it does."

"Home is always home and we always miss the town we grew up in," she said. "I'm so thankful I grew up here and never left."

The door swung open and our part-time help Lisa Anderson walked through the door. She was a high school student and helped several afternoons a week as well as weekends.

"Hi Lisa," I said, and popped the rest of the truffle into my mouth.

"Hi Mia, hi Mrs. Jordan. Did you hear about the fire?" She came around to the backside of the counter and stowed her purse in the lock drawer we had there.

"We did," I said with a frown.

"Everyone at school was talking about it. Is it true the farmhouse caught on fire?" she asked, picking up an apron and putting it over her neck.

"No, thank goodness. It was only the corn and straw mazes," I said. "The farmhouse and everything else are fine, but we lost the mazes and that's really going to hurt the Halloween season."

"My grandmother picked me up from school and she said we're having all these problems because of the curse," she said, leaning on the front counter.

"What curse are you talking about?" I glanced at my mother and she gave me a look that said something was up.

"My grandmother said a witch put a curse on Pumpkin Hollow back in 1892 when the town was first built. Every thirty years tragedy strikes and doesn't stop until the witch wakes up from the sleep she was cursed with and sacrifices someone for herself. We've had two murders and now the mazes have been set on fire," she said, nodding her head earnestly.

I looked at Lisa. She had short dark brown hair with a red ribbon in it. With her creamy complexion, she frequently dressed as Snow White on the weekends. This witch story sounded crazy and I couldn't imagine how anyone could believe it.

"Lisa, there's no such thing as witches and we are not cursed," I said. She was a smart girl and I couldn't imagine why she would believe such a thing.

"Mia, my grandmother has lived here all her life. The witch was an old woman that lived here on the mountain before anyone else and she didn't want a town built here. She's getting her revenge on us like she did the generations before us," she said, tying the apron behind her. "I think we all need to be careful."

I glanced up at the three customers that were in the shop. They had all turned in Lisa's direction and were listening intently.

"Lisa, that's an old wives' tale. Sometimes people make things up to liven up their lives," I said pointedly. The last thing we needed was for people to believe these wild tales and get scared off.

"My grandmother wouldn't make this up," she said, putting her hands on her hips. "She's lived here all her life. She said thirty years ago a little boy drowned in the creek outside of town and there were three murders. She also said there was a fire that burned down the old feed store."

"No, it's not your grandmother that's telling tales," I said, backpedaling. I didn't want to hurt her feelings, but her grandmother, Mrs. James, liked to talk and loved attention. She was a frequent customer with a penchant for peanut butter fudge, and had a tendency to over-dramatize every little thing that happened in town and then spread gossip about it. "What I mean is, she probably heard a rumor started by someone else. Right, Mom?"

Mom smiled. "Sometimes people's imaginations run away with them. Years ago there wasn't as much science behind police investigations, so it was hard to know exactly what had happened in the case of a murder. Or even an accident that didn't quite seem right," Mom said. "We've always been a family-oriented town with lots of fun activities for kids, Lisa. Accidents happen. Tragedies happen. I've lived here all my life and I can say without hesitation, there's no curse."

Mom said it loud enough for the customers to hear and they went back to looking over the candy.

"Well, my grandmother sure seems to believe it," Lisa said, sounding uncertain. "I better get to work cleaning."

I gave her a smile. "Thanks, Lisa," I said.

One of the customers stepped up to the cash register and I went to help her.

"Did you find everything okay?" I asked.

"I did," she said, putting a bag of taffy and three marzipan pumpkins on the counter. "I heard what she said about a curse. I don't believe in curses, but you know, sometimes bad things happen when bad things are spoken over someone or something."

I smiled. "I think it's just a few people that have an over-active imagination. I've never heard of any drowning or murder in the past."

She shrugged. "Is it true there have been some murders here recently?"

I looked at her. I wanted to lie, but I figured she'd hear it on the news. "We've had two people die. But prior to that, Pumpkin Hollow has been one of the safest, nicest towns you've ever seen."

She made a clucking sound. "It's the words you speak. Someone's saying bad things about this town."

"I'll keep that in mind," I said and rang up her purchases.

When she left I looked at my mother.

She shrugged. "It's not like you can keep it a secret. And we could all be a little more positive, if the truth be told."

"I'm going to be positive about business picking up then," I said with a chuckle.

"Two murders?" another customer asked, walking up to the front counter.

I smiled. "Yes, it's a shame. Can I help you with something?" I hated sounding like I was blowing her off, but I didn't want to upset anyone.

"I'd like four pumpkin truffles and a half pound of fudge with walnuts," she said. "I heard about those murders on the news. If I had kids, I wouldn't bring them here."

I went to the display case and opened it up. "There's nothing to worry about. This is completely out of the ordinary for us and we have a great police department that's working on keeping things safe."

"I still wouldn't bring small children here," she said. "I can't imagine how frightening it would be for them."

I put her truffles in a wax paper bag and folded the top over. What I wanted to say was that just because someone had a grudge against someone and killed them, it didn't mean everyone that visited the town was at risk, but I kept my mouth shut. People were going to believe what they wanted to believe.

"Here we are," I said, after cutting a half-pound of fudge for her and putting it into another bag. "The best fudge and truffles in the state. We make them by hand with only the freshest ingredients." When trying to keep someone from talking about an unpleasant subject, I found it best to change the subject. And there was no better subject than chocolate.

"I love your fudge and truffles. I can't get enough of them," she said. "Sorry if I seemed rude a minute ago. Murder is just a scary thing."

I nodded and rang up her purchases. "We have the best police force in the state and I know they'll catch whoever committed the murder. The person that murdered the first victim is behind bars, by the way."

"I'm glad to hear that," she said and ran her debit card though the card reader. "I hope they find the other murderer."

"I know they will."

I sighed inwardly. Would customers be too scared to come to Pumpkin Hollow? I glanced at Lisa. We didn't need the customers getting spooked by wild tales.

Chapter Nine

"Mom, if you had to guess, who would you say murdered the mayor?" I asked, when I got her alone in the back room.

She smiled. "Now, that's the question of the day, isn't it? I really don't know. I can't think of anyone in particular and I keep wondering why someone would even want to kill him. But then I start counting the reasons. He possibly embezzled from the high school, he wanted to end the Halloween season and thereby end some of the businesses, and he wasn't a particularly likeable person. I'm sure there are a dozen reasons I haven't even thought of."

I nodded. It was all true, especially the part about not being particularly likeable. No one wanted him for a teacher when I was in school.

"Mom, is what Lisa said true? Were there other murders? And what about a drowning and a fire?" I asked.

"There were, but it wasn't because of a curse," she said, measuring sugar into a deep saucepan. "The Johnson boy wandered off when his family went on a picnic. There were a lot of cousins and aunts and uncles and somehow they lost track of the boy. It was a real tragedy. A very sad day for everyone that knew the family."

"What about the three murders?" I asked.

"Well, that was something else. The police never could figure out what happened. They found some college kids out in the woods. They had gone out there to party, but according to the other kids that were at the party, everyone left about the same time. For some reason, the three went back out into the woods, but no one knows why. The police said they died of alcohol poisoning, but a rumor got started that they had been murdered. The other kids at the party insisted foul play was involved, but there wasn't enough evidence to suggest that," she said and poured cream into the saucepan.

"And the fire at the feed store?"

She shook her head. "I don't believe the fire marshal ever figured it out. Like I said before, the science may not have been there thirty years ago. Or maybe there just wasn't enough evidence."

I rolled my eyes. "I don't know why people jump to conclusions about these things. If it gets around there's a curse or that there have been previous deaths, people won't want to come to Pumpkin Hollow."

Mom shrugged. "Or we could play up the curse. It is a Halloween-themed town, after all. Some people enjoy being scared."

"Seriously?" I asked her. "We've always been so family-oriented."

She shrugged and turned the stove burner on. "I don't think it will bother most people. Maybe a few. But everyone knows none of it's real. It's for entertainment. And you know what they say to do when life hands you lemons."

She was probably right. I was making too much of trying to protect the town from the rumors. Maybe it was time to change in order to save the town. A scarier outlook might be just what we needed.

THE NEXT DAY I DROVE over to the elementary school at lunchtime. I had made plans to catch up with an old friend, Jennifer Scott, and I picked up a Hawaiian pizza on the way. Jennifer and I had been friends most of our lives. She had gone to college and become a teacher, while I had lingered in school long enough to earn three master's degrees. Let's just say I had issues with decision-making.

"Jennifer!" I said, standing in the doorway to her now empty third grade classroom.

"Mia!" she said, looking up from a stack of papers on her desk.

I hurried over to her and set the pizza on her desk. She came around the side and gave me a hug.

"You haven't changed a bit," I said. And she hadn't. Jennifer had long, straight, auburn hair and blue eyes that lit up when she smiled.

"You haven't either," she said. "I'm so glad you moved back to Pumpkin Hollow. We have so much to catch up on. Have a seat." She motioned toward a child's chair sitting at the side of her desk. "The kids will be at lunch for another thirty minutes."

I laughed at the chair. "This brings back memories."

"Sorry, they only give us one grownup chair," she said and sat down in hers.

"It's fine. I've always looked up to you, anyway," I giggled. "I brought some paper plates and napkins. Oh, and a bottle of root beer." I pulled the chilled two-liter bottle from my bag and set it on the table along with two plastic cups.

"My goodness, you do come prepared," she said, and opened the lid to the pizza box.

"Yes, I do," I said, sitting on the mini chair. "So, tell me what's new with you."

"I'm engaged!" she said with a squeal, and held her hand out for me to see the ring. "Chad Rhoades."

I gasped. "Jennifer, I'm so happy for you! What a beautiful ring!" I said. And I really was happy for her. Mostly. But to tell the truth, I'd have to say my heart sank just a tiny bit. My best friend, Amanda Krigbaum, was engaged to my ex-boyfriend from high school, Brian Shoate. Now Jennifer was engaged to our class valedictorian, Chad Rhoades. All I had to show for my ten years post high school graduation was three master's degrees I might never use, and the same job I had in high school.

"Thanks, Mia. I still have to pinch myself every now and then. What about you? Are you seeing anyone?" she asked, picking up a slice of pizza and putting it on one of the paper plates.

I paused a moment, then shook my head. "Nope. No one."

"Well, don't worry about that. Your Prince Charming is coming, I just know it. You're too cute to be alone long," she said.

I nodded, and hoped it was true. "Thanks, Jennifer. So, did you hear about the mayor's death?" Dating wasn't a subject I was comfortable with, so I changed the subject to be safe.

She nodded, taking a bite of her pizza. "Terrible," she said around the pizza in her mouth.

"The pizza?" I asked, peering at the rest of it in the box.

"No, the mayor being killed," she clarified. "It's kind of scary having two murders in this town in less than a month."

"It really is," I said, picking up a slice of pizza from the box. "I remember him from high school. He wasn't my favorite teacher, but he didn't deserve to die like that."

"I doubt he was anyone's favorite teacher," she said.

"I heard a rumor that there was some missing fundraiser money. Is that true?" I asked, lowering my voice. "You can tell me if I'm being nosy."

Even though Jennifer was at the elementary school, I knew teachers were a tight group. Someone had to know something. At least, I hoped that was the case.

Her eyebrows went up. "The high school is keeping a tight lid on that one. It was a hot rumor for a while and had everyone talking. But no one knows for sure what happened."

I nodded. "I just thought someone might have talked about it and spilled the beans."

"That's what usually happens," she said, pouring a cup of root beer. "Everyone talks, but for some reason in this case, no one seemed to know what really happened. Judging from the fact that the glee club didn't go to regionals, I'd say it had to be true. But Stan Goodall told everyone they just didn't raise enough money and what little they raised was put into a fund."

"How do you know that isn't true?" I asked.

"Because in this school district, there aren't any funds like that. Money is always in short supply and that money was earmarked for a special purpose. It would have been used right away for something else for the glee club."

"Did he retire from the high school?" I asked. "With honors?"

She looked at me a moment, then laughed. "Come on, Mia. No one would think he retired from the high school with honors. What happened is that he was retired against his will. Besides, what does retiring with honors even mean?"

I laughed. It had sounded odd when Jerry Crownover had insisted it was true, and now Jennifer was confirming there was no such thing. "Do you know for sure that he was retired against his will?"

"There were other complaints. No one liked him at the high school except his wife and she was a librarian with no pull. He was retired, trust me," she said.

"What other complaints?" I asked.

"This is between you and me, okay?" she said, leaning in.

"Of course," I assured her.

"Apparently there was a student that had a crush on him. They swore nothing ever happened, and that's probably true, but when rumors start, it's hard to stop them. And then there's the little problem of kids not liking him. He always had parents calling on behalf of their kids because something or other happened in class. He didn't speak very nicely to the kids. Not exactly a nice guy, you know?"

I nodded. "I remember him yelling at Don Brand for not bringing his book to class. He kind of lost control and screamed at him," I said, thinking back. "Do you know who the student with the crush was?"

"Nope. The high school kept a lid on that, too. When you add the missing funds to an already troubled career, it was just easier for the district to get rid of him before something worse happened."

It was something to think about. I knew Stan Goodall wasn't a popular teacher, and had even seen him lose his temper a couple of times, so I wasn't surprised he got a lot of complaints. But he was middle-aged, balding and had a pot belly, along with an unpleasant personality. I couldn't imagine a student having a crush on him. It made me wonder who that student was, and if whoever it was still lived in town.

Chapter Ten

I stood on Ethan's doorstep, with my hand poised to knock. My stomach did a little flip-flop and I breathed in deeply.

This is not a date.

Ethan had stopped by the candy store after his shift ended this afternoon and asked if I wanted to drop by his house for pizza and to discuss strategies to bring business in to town. I had butterflies at the thought of being alone with him at his house.

Not a date, I reminded myself.

I knocked on the door. Ethan lived in a neat little cottage in the middle of town. There were twelve little houses that looked exactly alike, painted white with black shutters, on Pumpkin Lane. Six of the houses were on one side of the street and six more across the street. I had always admired these little houses with their cute little window boxes and black shutters and I wondered if any of them were for rent. At twenty-eight, it was time I had my own place.

Ethan answered the door with a smile. "Hey, Mia, I'm glad you came. Come on in."

I followed him into the living room and he offered me a seat on the sofa. I looked around the room. Ethan's style was thrown-together items that didn't exactly match, but didn't clash, either. The sofa was tan with dark wood trim and the loveseat was dark brown, matching the wood accents on the sofa.

"You have a nice place here," I said. "I'm glad you stopped by this afternoon. Getting together to discuss ways to drum up more business is a great idea."

He chuckled. "I'm not much on decorating, and to be honest, some of this furniture is what my parents gave me when I moved out of their house after high school."

"It's great," I said. "I like it. I've been thinking I need to get my own place. Living at home at my age feels kind of weird."

"Parents cramping your style?" he asked with a raised eyebrow.

I laughed. "No. I don't have a style. I'm just too old to be living with them and I really should look for a place of my own."

"I completely understand. Can I get you something to drink?"

"Water would be great," I said.

"What kind of pizza do you want?" he asked as he disappeared into the kitchen.

"Hawaiian. It's my favorite and I could eat it every day of the week," I answered, looking around and taking in more of the living room. On the bookcase there was a picture of him and a girl I didn't know. Did Ethan have a girlfriend? He hadn't mentioned one and now I was feeling a little uncomfortable. Would she be upset he had invited a woman over for dinner without including her?

"Here you go," he said and handed me a bottle of water. He picked up a tablet off the coffee table and ran his finger over the screen. "And we'll have pizza shortly."

"Thanks, Ethan," I said. I wondered how I could bring up the picture without seeming like I was snooping into his personal life. "Was anything found at the fire site?" I asked, instead.

"Not really. I did see the fire marshal bag up a couple of things, but I wasn't close enough to see exactly what it was."

"Have you lived in this house long?" I asked, glancing at the picture.

"This is my first and only house I've lived in on my own," he said and set the tablet down on the coffee table. "It's a nice, quiet neighborhood."

"Your squad car parked out front wouldn't have anything to do with that, would it?" I asked.

He grinned. "I'm sure it helps."

"So, who's going to take over as mayor?" I asked. "What's the contingency plan for a murdered mayor?" I had been thinking about that. I wasn't sure how things worked.

"Somebody on the city council, I think," he said, twisting off the top of a bottle of water.

I nodded, thinking over the choices we were faced with. "I wonder how the city council feels about the Halloween season?"

"I've heard rumors that most of them are against it," Ethan said. "But you never can tell."

I groaned. "Great. That's just what we don't need."

"It could be just rumors. People talk a lot," he assured me. "The last thing we need to do is give up hope."

"I know, you're right. Sometimes small town living has its drawbacks though."

Ethan chuckled. "Sometimes it does."

"I'm sure Jerry Crownover will be more determined than ever to stop the Halloween season," I said, taking a sip of my water. "I don't know why it matters so much to him. He hasn't lived here that long."

Ethan nodded. "I think we may have more trouble with him now that his brother-in-law has been murdered."

I didn't want to think about it. We had enough to worry about, now that the mazes were gone and rumors were flying about curses, murders, and fires.

"Lisa, our part-time help, came in this afternoon and said her grandmother told her Pumpkin Hollow was under a curse. Every thirty years forces will come against the town and people die and fires start."

Ethan looked at me with a blank face for a minute. Then he started laughing. "Wow, a curse. Just what we needed. That's funny."

"It is, but if it spreads it might scare tourists off. The ones in the candy store that heard her tell my mom and me about it, got a little worried," I said.

He shook his head. "That's crazy. Okay, well, we've got a murder, an arson fire, and now a curse. What next?"

"Not just any curse. A witch's curse," I informed him.

He rolled his eyes. "I'll keep an eye out for errant witches when I'm on duty. And why does the curse manifest every thirty years? Why not fifty? Or twenty-five?"

I shrugged. "Maybe thirty means something in a witch's world."

"Where are Dorothy and the Tin Man when you need them?" he asked with a chuckle.

"In better news, the town website is doing well with several hundred more visits since last weekend. I wish the city council would make it more official. I feel like a rogue Webmaster without their approval."

"I wouldn't worry about it. You're really just advertising the seasonal businesses and you have a right to do that, especially since your parents own a business."

"I guess so," I said. "We've had a lot of hits on it. I feel very hopeful that business will improve. Actually, it has improved at the candy store. I told my mother we needed to create a website to sell our candy. I think if we beef up our internet presence, we can sell candy all over the country."

"That's a great idea," he said, smiling. "So tell me, how are things for you since you got back? Are you glad you made the move?"

I smiled at him. "I am happy to be back. It's better than I remembered. I feel like something good is about to happen, in spite of the murders and the fire. I don't know why I feel that way, but I do."

"That's great. I agree with you. With the ideas everyone's contributing to increase business, I do think things are going to improve around here. What about personally? Have you been catching up with old friends?"

"Amanda and a couple of girls from school," I said, wondering where this was going.

"That's it? Just some girls from school?" he asked, watching me closely.

I shrugged. "They're nice girls from school and I'm happy to get back together with them." I gave him a Cheshire cat grin.

"No guys from school?" he asked, raising one eyebrow.

"Nope. Not a one," I said, and took another sip of water. "Well, there's my ex-boyfriend Brian Shoate, but he seems to be busy with Amanda. They're engaged, in case you haven't heard."

"I have heard that. I'm happy for them. I would have thought you would have looked up other old boyfriends," he said.

My eyes met his. Where was he going with this?

The doorbell rang and we both looked at the door.

"Saved by the bell," he muttered and went to answer it.

I smiled to myself. What was Ethan up to? Ethan had been the cutest boy in school and had never paid much attention to me before now.

"That was fast," I said to his back.

"Pizza!" Ethan exclaimed, as he came back and put the pizza box on the coffee table.

"I'm starving. I hope there's enough for you," I said.

"Let me get some plates and napkins," he said and disappeared into the kitchen.

I opened the top of the pizza box and my stomach growled. I had pizza for lunch the day before, but I was addicted to it and could eat it every day.

"It smells wonderful," I said when Ethan came back with the plates.

"Pizza Town makes the best pizza in town. Hence, the name. It may be the best in the state," he said. He handed me a plate and waited for me to help myself. "Since you haven't reacquainted yourself with any old boyfriends from school, maybe we could go out to dinner one night."

I froze mid-pizza cut. "That sounds like a good plan." I said after getting my thoughts together.

Did Ethan Banks really just ask me out?

"A real meal out. Not pizza," he said, grinning. "One of those fancy places where people actually serve you."

I nodded, and put the piece of pizza on my plate and sat back. "That sounds like fun. We could do that." I hoped I sounded calm, because I was anything but that on the inside.

He chuckled. "You're supposed to comment on my being cute. A fancy restaurant where they serve you. Ha ha."

I looked up at him, taking in what he was saying. I was still shocked that he had asked me out. "Ha ha," I finally said.

He shook his head and grinned at me. "How about Saturday night?"

I stared at him. Was I really going to go on a date with Ethan Banks?

"Mia?"

"Oh. There's a party at the Halloween party house on Saturday. Andrea's singing. Maybe we could go there?"

"Andrea's singing? That sounds great," he said.

I nodded. "Andrea can really sing. She has a fantastic voice," I said.

I stared at him. I had a date with Ethan Banks. Sixteen-year-old me would have run through the halls of our high school, screaming out the news. But adult me decided to act cool. Or at least, as cool as I was capable of acting.

Chapter Eleven

I was walking on air the next day as I headed to the costume shop to find a new outfit for the weekend. I had brought down a box with old costumes from the attic and gone through them, tossing some of the smaller ones. Apparently I had filled out a little since high school. I still had four cute ones, but I wanted something new.

I know a costume isn't most girls' choice of attire for a first date, but this was Pumpkin Hollow and wearing a costume wouldn't raise eyebrows. Plus, we were going to a Halloween party.

I pushed the door open and entered the Little Shop of Costumes. There were displays of werewolf, vampire and ghost costumes along one wall. Some of the masks were horror style and I didn't want anything like that. I preferred sweet costumes.

There was a rack in the middle of the shop with dresses and I went to it, flipping through the dresses on hangers.

"Hey, Miss Mia," Fagan said, coming from the back room.

"Hi Fagan," I said. "How are you?"

"I'm doing fine. The mayor's dead and I couldn't ask for much more."

I sighed, but didn't look up at him. "Now, Fagan, we need to be nice. Customers are looking for a happy experience, not a murderous one."

"Hey, I had nothing to do with anyone's murder. I'm just happy he's gone. And my being happy should make customers happy, right?"

"You do know someone will be taking over as mayor, and they may not support the Halloween season, don't you?" I asked, taking a princess costume off the rack and holding it up.

It was pink with lots of rhinestones and glitter. It was cute, but not quite me. Besides that, this was a first date and something about the princess costume said "steady relationship."

I put the princess costume back and picked up a gypsy costume. It had a green skirt and a brown top with a green and yellow scarf to wear. It came complete with four bead necklaces, six beaded bracelets and a pair of giant gold hoop earrings.

"I guess we'll just have to deal with that if it happens," Fagan said, becoming serious.

"That's what I thought," I said. "I'm sure everything will work out."

Fagan snorted. "I know things will work out. There's no way I'm going to just sit back and let some city council jerks make up laws that ruin everything good about this town."

"I don't know anything about small town politics, but I agree that we should stand up for our rights," I said, holding the costume up to myself to see if it would fit. There was a mirror along one wall and I walked over to it.

"Small town politics include passing laws to help people that are crooked. Don't think for a minute it's for the betterment of the town," he said, leaning against the front counter.

I shrugged. "I guess we'll just have to wait and see. As long as we get to keep celebrating the Halloween season, I'll be satisfied."

The gypsy costume was cute, but a little darker than I usually went. I liked it, though. I could see myself wearing the scarf over my head with a few tendrils of hair hanging loose.

"Wait and see," Fagan muttered. "Maybe we'll get lucky and someone will kill the new mayor, too."

I gasped. "Fagan, how can you say that? That's a terrible thing to say, no matter how much you disliked the mayor or anyone else."

"The guy was a jerk. There's no way you can get around that," he said, and sat down on a stool behind the counter. "That costume is twenty percent off."

"Even better," I said. "I think you've just made a sale."

The bell over the door jingled and we both turned toward the door. Andrea Stone walked in and she smiled when she saw me.

"Hi Mia, that's a cute costume," she said. "Are you going to get it?"

"I think I might," I said. "Especially since it's on sale. What are you up to?"

She headed over to the rack I had pulled the gypsy costume from. "It's time I bought a new costume. I have that gig at the Halloween party house and the few costumes I have are wearing thin. I need something new."

"Twenty percent off for people that work in the Halloween district," Fagan said from his spot leaning against the front counter. "I figure we should support one another."

"That's a great idea, Fagan. I'll talk to my mom about doing that. Maybe we can get all the businesses to offer a discount to one another to encourage spending among ourselves."

"Sounds like a plan," he said.

"I heard about the fire," Andrea said, looking through the costumes. "I can't imagine who would do that."

"I know, it's terrible," I said.

"If you ask me, I think the murderer did it," Fagan said. "They wanted to destroy evidence."

Andrea looked at Fagan and then at me. "Do you think so?"

I shrugged. "Anything's possible, I guess. It's a shame. We really needed those mazes for business."

"I don't think the murderer burned the mazes," Andrea said, shaking her head. "It doesn't make sense."

"What do you mean it doesn't make sense?" Fagan said. "What better way to get rid of evidence?"

Andrea looked at Fagan. "Well, don't you think if the killer was going to do it, he would have done it when he killed the mayor? I mean, I'm just thinking that might seem more logical."

"You might have a point," I said, laying the gypsy costume on the front counter. "I know the police went over the corn maze when they found the mayor's body, but it was a big maze. They might not have gotten everything."

"What kind of evidence did they find?" Andrea asked. "Did Ethan tell you?"

"No, I don't think he can talk about that kind of stuff. Or maybe he can, I'm not sure. But he hasn't mentioned it. I just know they searched the maze," I said.

"Oh," Andrea said, nodding. "Of course they did. That's the first thing they would do. You have to wonder if they really knew what they were doing, though."

"What do you mean?" I asked.

She shrugged, and held up the same princess costume I had looked at earlier. "Small town police force. No offense, Ethan's great, but the rest of them? I doubt they would know how to properly search for clues."

I could feel my hackles rise just a little. I hadn't had my first date with Ethan yet, but I already felt protective of him.

"I bet they're doing just fine. Trying to solve a crime is hard, I'm sure."

"I still think the killer set fire to the corn maze," Fagan interrupted. "Maybe the killer went back and realized there was something he had left behind and he set it on fire." He rang up my costume and put it into a bag.

I paid for my costume and turned back to Andrea. She stared back at me, her face pale.

"Are you okay, Andrea?" I asked.

"What? Of course," she said and smiled. "I just hate that we lost the mazes. I hope it doesn't hurt business too much."

"We'll come up with something else," I assured her. "We need to get something in line soon."

"I heard there's a rumor of a curse," Andrea suddenly said. "I heard the fire, Hazel Martin's death, and the mayor's murder happened because of a curse. I know that sounds crazy, but maybe there's some truth to it?"

"Sorry, but I don't believe in that kind of thing. There's no such thing as witches or curses. It's a Halloween town, but not a cursed town," I said with a chuckle. I couldn't understand how some people were so quick to think something like a curse existed. It was silly.

Fagan chuckled. "A curse. What we need is a witch to cast a spell on everyone that wants to vote against the Halloween season. Maybe she could make them all vote in its favor."

"Now, that would be awesome. We could just make everyone get behind the season and we would have it made. Well, I've got to get going. Thanks for the discount, Fagan."

"You're welcome, Mia. Tell your mom to come down and buy something. I've gotten some new costumes and accessories in," Fagan said.

"I'll do that," I said, and headed toward the door. "Andrea, I'll see you this weekend. And don't worry about curses. People talk about that kind of stuff, but it's just overactive imaginations at work."

"I know, I'm not worried," Andrea said. She put the princess costume back on the rack and went back to looking through the other costumes.

I pushed the door open and walked out into the sunshine. I smiled and looked around at all the decorated shops. The gift shop across the street had cute orange pumpkins painted around the edges of the big picture window in front and the flower shop next door had a brightly painted goblin statue out front holding a jack-o-lantern with orange and purple flowers in it.

I smiled. I loved the Halloween season. As I stood admiring the decorated shops, a large black cloud floated across the sky, blotting out the sun, and a cool breeze blew in. I looked up and sighed.

There's no curse.

Chapter Twelve

Saturday morning dawned clear and bright. I put on my black cat costume and got ready for work. I was saving the gypsy costume for the party later this evening. I couldn't risk getting chocolate or anything else on the front.

I was in the candy shop kitchen, working on popcorn balls. I dropped some red and yellow food coloring into the syrup as soon as I took it off the heat, and then poured it into a huge vat of popcorn I had made earlier.

Using a rubber spatula, I stirred and turned the popcorn until it was coated. I put some plastic gloves on and picked up a bit of butter and rubbed it over the gloves, then began shaping the popcorn into balls. I had done it so many times, it had become instinctive to know how much went into each ball. I was an expert at making perfectly sized and shaped popcorn balls. I set each one on a cooling rack and began another.

Mom popped into the kitchen as I was finishing up.

"Hey, Mom. Popcorn balls are ready."

"Wonderful," she said, tying her apron on. "Love the kitty costume."

"Thanks. What are you going to make?" I asked.

"It's a surprise," she said. "If you'll go out front and wait on customers, I'll bring a treat out to you."

"That sounds promising," I said.

I washed up and went out front to lean on the front counter, wondering why we didn't have any customers yet when Stella Moretti walked through the door.

"I need pumpkin fudge," she said. Stella owned the Sweet Goblin Bakery two blocks down the street.

"Hi Stella, how are you?" I asked, opening the display case.

"Great. I need a half pound," she said. She wore black slacks and a blue top. Stella wasn't much on Halloween. She should have been since she owned a bakery in the Halloween business district, but she wanted to end the Halloween season along with a few of the other business owners.

"So Stella, how's business been?" I asked as I cut a slab of fudge for her.

"The same as it's always been," she said, looking over the rest of the candy in the display case.

"Really? You haven't seen an increase in business since the season began?" I asked.

She shrugged. "Maybe a little. What does it matter? I hate the Halloween season. I want it to end."

"Stella, we have such a wonderful opportunity here to do something different. Why don't you just play along?"

"Like I haven't played along all these years? Can I just have my fudge?" she said, digging through her purse for her debit card.

I sighed and put her fudge into a wax paper bag and then into a cute Halloween paper bag. I loved Halloween and Stella Moretti wasn't going to drag me down.

"Here you go," I said, and handed her the bag, then rang her up.

"Great. Thanks, kid," she said and ran her debit card through the card reader. I wanted to bring up the Halloween season vote but I figured it would get me nowhere. She wasn't going to budge on where she stood with the Halloween season.

"See you later," I said as she pushed the door open and left. I sat on a stool behind the counter and thought about what had happened in the past few weeks. I hoped the fire and the murder weren't going to hurt our business.

"Look what I made," Mom said, coming out of the kitchen with a tray of candy.

I gasped. "Are those homemade marshmallows?"

"They are. I made them candy corn flavored. They turned out pretty well," she said, opening the display case.

"I've got to try one," I said and snitched one off the tray. I popped it into my mouth and I was not disappointed. "Wow, Mom, this is good. I mean, really good."

"Don't talk with your mouth full, dear," she said, using tongs to put the marshmallows into the display case.

"I can't help it. You got the flavor down perfectly," I said. The marshmallow was square in shape and light yellow. She had dipped the bottom in chocolate and it melted in my mouth.

"Good. I'm glad you like them. I hope they sell well," she said. "It's been slow today."

"I know, but I'm sure it will pick up," I said. "You know what I was thinking? I want to experiment with some cupcakes. We can make some cute ones that we decorate with candy."

Mom gave me a look. "Don't you think Stella Moretti will be up in arms about that? We sell candy and she sells the baked goods."

"She hates the Halloween season and hardly bakes anything Halloween themed anymore. There's no law that says there can't be competition. It's a business, after all."

She shrugged. "You know how Stella is. If you want to deal with her, be my guest. It might bring in more business."

"It would be wonderful for business," I agreed. "I think I'm going to take a walk around and see if anyone else is doing any business. Do you mind?"

"No, go ahead. Lisa will be in pretty soon," she said.

The weather was cooler this morning and I relished it. I loved fall and I was more than ready for it to start. Tourists wandered the sidewalks, looking into shop windows, and that made me feel better. They would wander into the candy shop at some point during the day. A visit to Pumpkin Hollow wasn't complete without stopping in at the candy store.

"Hey Mike," I said to the mummy walking toward me. He groaned in response. I loved the characters wandering around on the weekends. People stopped and took pictures with them. That was one of the best parts of living in a Halloween town. Halloween was everywhere.

Up ahead of me I saw Martha Mayes, the president of the homeowners association, dressed as a witch. She cackled when talking to a family of four. The kids looked to be ten and twelve and were almost too old to be scared, but they hung back, not quite sure. Martha held her hand out to shake the older boy's hand and after a moment's hesitation, he reached his hand out to her.

The family continued down the sidewalk and I headed toward Martha.

"Hey, Martha, how are things going?" I asked her. Her face was covered in green makeup and she wore a prosthetic nose with a wart on the end.

"Really good. People love seeing a witch wandering the town. Oh, except for the one that cast a spell on the town," she said in her own voice. "How are you doing?"

"I'm good. There are no real witches," I pointed out.

She laughed. "I know, but people are going to believe what they're going to believe."

"Do you think the crowds are as large as they normally are?" I asked.

"It does seem like the crowds are a little thin this morning, but it's early yet. They'll be here," she said, adjusting her hat.

"I hope so," I said. "Mom made a new recipe this morning. Candy corn flavored marshmallows if you're interested."

"Oh, that sounds good," she said. Her eyes lit up and she smiled. "I'll have to stop by."

"Let me know how you like them. See you later," I said and headed toward the haunted house. It was opening day for the haunted house and I hoped to see a long line there.

Up ahead I saw Susan Goodall with her brother, Jerry. They had their backs to me and appeared to be deep in conversation. When I got closer, I realized they were arguing.

"Don't you lay that one on me," Jerry hissed. "I had nothing to do with that."

"You had nothing to do with it? Are you kidding me? It was your big idea," Susan said. "If you had thought it out a little more, things would have gone smoother."

I stopped in my tracks. I didn't mean to eavesdrop, but they were blocking the sidewalk.

Jerry suddenly spun around and faced me. "What do you want?" he barked.

"To pass by," I said calmly.

Jerry's face was red. "Sorry," he said and they moved aside so I could pass.

I continued toward the haunted house, and resisted the temptation to look back at them. Whatever they were discussing seemed important. Did it have something to do with Stan's murder? I needed to talk to Ethan.

I turned the corner and could hear the haunted house playing its creepy music. I smiled. One thing you could count on was the haunted house being a huge draw. The sound track was the same every year, creaking boards, chains being dragged, a few wolf howls and a little scary organ music punctuated by screams in the distance. I loved it.

A few people sat on the wrought iron benches out front as the haunted house loomed over them. The house had originally been a Victorian mansion with a tall clock tower, built in the late 1800s. It had been empty for years when the town took on the Halloween theme and the owner transformed it into a haunted house. The house had had several upgrades through the years.

I stood on the corner and admired it. Black spider webs clung to the corners of the dusty windows and a large black spider made its way down the front porch. The clapboard siding was a peeling white-turned-gray color and added to the creep factor. A wrought iron fence surrounded the property and the gates were wide open now to accommodate tourists.

A man in a stovepipe top hat with an 1800s style black coat, and black shoes with white spats, sat on a chair near the entrance. His head was tilted downward and he remained still, until a group of people made their way to the front door. Then he would reach out a hand and touch someone's arm, or he would stay still and groan as people passed. Anything to get a reaction out of the tourists.

I smiled as a group of four teenagers walked up to the wide black door and he jumped to his feet and screamed. The kids screamed and three ran through the door, with one backing up down the porch. The man in black sat back on the chair as the teen's friends coaxed the scared teen into the house. He shook his head. Then the man in black looked at him and motioned him forward.

Brett Stevens played the man in black and he was a nice guy when not in costume. I grinned, watching the scene before me. Brett coaxed the young teen and the teen ran through the entrance to the haunted house, Brett letting him by without further hassle.

I walked across the street and headed to the entrance of the haunted house. The haunted house was traditional, with a lot of ghouls jumping out to scare people and some creepy things to look at. Not much else happened in there, no chainsaws or mass murderers, just good clean scares. It was what people enjoyed about the haunted house.

A small line was forming at the ticket booth and I went to talk to Marilyn Jones, who played a witch hanging out at the front of the haunted house. She got paid to cackle at people, which wasn't a bad gig if you could get it.

"Hi, Marilyn, how are things going?" I asked.

"Not bad. Maybe a little slow, but still not bad," she said, and cackled.

"That's good to hear," I said.

I walked toward the tourists waiting out front. There was a ticket booth at an open window on the side of the house and a shorter than expected line of people waiting to buy a ticket.

"I heard there's been a lot of murders here," one woman said as she waited in line.

"I heard there were nine so far this year. I don't think we should have come," another said, looking over her shoulder nervously.

I swallowed hard. *Nine?* Where were these people getting their gossip?

"Hi everyone," I said. "How are you enjoying your visit?"

They turned and looked at me. I was harmless in my cat costume.

"Is it true about the murders?" the lady who said there were nine murders asked.

"No, there haven't been nine murders. Pumpkin Hollow has one of the lowest crime rates in California and we pride ourselves on being a family-friendly town." I smiled and didn't mention the recent murders. "If you have time after enjoying the haunted house, you might want to stop by the Pumpkin Hollow Candy Store. My parents own it and my mother just whipped up a batch of homemade candy corn marshmallows. They're dipped in chocolate and are absolutely wonderful."

"That sounds really good," she said.

"I always stop at the candy shop. It's one of my favorite places," another said.

I gave them a big smile. "I'm so glad to hear that. Enjoy the activities and have fun!"

I moved on before they could ask about the murders. I hadn't lied, I had just forgotten to mention the two murders we had had this year. It was a fluke and there was no reason to allow it to tarnish the town's reputation.

I turned and watched a group of about a dozen middle school kids and three chaperones heading toward the haunted house. Pumpkin Hollow was on its way back.

Chapter Thirteen

We arrived at the Halloween party at seven sharp. I wore my gypsy costume with the scarf tied over my head. My hair was long with a little bit of curl, but I had given it some extra curl. As I looked in the mirror when I was getting dressed, I had wondered if I should have colored it black with a temporary colorant, but it was too late to do it then. I had to admit, I made a pretty good gypsy.

People milled about in front of the house. It had a similar look to the haunted house, with dusty windows and spider webs in the corners of the windows. The front façade was made to look like a two-story Victorian house with a turret. What looked like the second floor of the house was actually an attic for the single level house and was used for storage of props. I had been through all of the Halloween houses and events at one time or another in my life and I knew all their secrets.

"Ready to go inside?" Ethan asked.

"Sure," I said. I was nervous about our first date and I was glad we were going to be at a party with a lot of other people. Sometimes I became tongue-tied when I was nervous and having something other than Ethan to focus on might help me stay calm.

Ethan had dressed as a vampire, complete with black cape and fake fangs. He slicked his blond hair back, making a dashing vampire.

Gigantic jack-o-lanterns graced the porch area next to the front door where we entered. Every nook and cranny of the house was decorated. Most of the decorations were vintage or vintage inspired. A long table was set out with candy, made by my mother and myself, finger foods, candy apples, and an assortment of desserts. Two large punch bowls were filled with red punch and frozen eyeballs floated in it to keep it cold.

"Hi Mia," Andrea gushed and ran up to us. "Hi Ethan, hi Mia! I can't believe I got a job singing for the party!"

"You'll do great, Andrea. I can't wait to see you perform," I said. Andrea was one of the best singers I'd ever heard and I still thought she should try out on one of those television talent search shows.

"Congratulations on the new job," Ethan told her. "You make a beautiful princess."

"You do," I agreed. She was wearing the same princess costume I had seen at Fagan's costume shop. It looked great on her and I was glad I didn't buy it. It was made her.

"Thanks," she said. "I gotta go now. See you both later."

I laughed. "She's so cute," I said to Ethan.

"Yes, she is. And you make a pretty cute Gypsy too," he said, smiling at me.

I felt myself blush. "Thanks. I like your vampire costume, too. They did a great job decorating in here, didn't they?" I said, changing the subject.

"They did," he said and chuckled. "It always looks nice in here."

Ethan had swoon-worthy blue eyes. I had to remind myself not to stare into them too deeply. I didn't want to freak him out.

"I'm having a good time," I said lamely.

He grinned. "Me too."

Ethan was making me nervous, so I looked around the room at the decorations and tried to act natural. Angela Peterson and her husband Phil owned the party houses and they changed up the decorations every year. This year they had gone with a black theme with purple accents. Witches, vampires, and mummy props and decorations abounded. I kept my eye on the decorations to keep from looking at Ethan. I wasn't sure why I was feeling so shy.

"Hey guys," Amanda said, walking up in a slinky witch costume. "There are a lot of people here. That's great to see."

"It is," I said. "It's exciting."

"You make a terrific witch, Amanda," Ethan said.

"Back at ya, Count," she said and laughed.

As the room filled with people, Andrea went to the stage at the front of the room. There was a small band and they began playing. Andrea opened her mouth and the magic began as she sang an old Hollywood movie musical tune. She had the perfect voice to draw you back into the 1940s and make you stop and listen. I couldn't imagine being able to sing like that. It was wonderful.

"Care for some punch?" Ethan asked, bending down and speaking near my ear.

I nodded and followed him over to the table. People hovered nearby, filling their plates with tiny sandwiches. Ethan picked up a clear plastic cup and using the dipper, poured punch into it and handed it to me.

"Thanks," I said and took a sip. The punch was strawberry flavored and Ethan had put a frozen grape eyeball into it for me.

There was a bar in an adjoining room for more adult beverages, but I had never been a drinker and I hoped Ethan wasn't, either. It occurred to me that I really didn't know a lot about him. He poured himself a cup of punch and we moved off to a corner of the room.

"So, tell me about your life since high school," I said over the music. I leaned against the wall and he moved in close to talk to me.

He shrugged. "I dated a lawyer that moved to town for two years. She got bored and moved away, leaving my little broken heart behind," he said with a grin. "Other than that, I've been a police officer since I graduated from the academy."

"Aw, I'm sorry. Was it a serious relationship?" I asked.

"I thought so. But she had other thoughts, I guess. She packed up her office and was gone two days later."

"Wow," I said. "I don't know how a lawyer would have enough business to make a living in this town."

"She didn't. She moved here because her grandparents died and left her a house. The Livingstons. Do you remember them?" he asked.

I nodded. "Yeah, I remember them," I said. I looked up into Ethan's eyes. They sparkled in the dimmed lighting. I smiled at him. He had gone from cute schoolboy to handsome gentleman while I had been away.

I could see the door from where I leaned and Fagan Branigan walked through it with his wife following behind him. Neither had dressed up. They headed over to the room with the bar and disappeared into it.

Ethan watched them go.

"You don't suspect him, do you?" I asked, lowering my voice.

He turned back to me and shrugged. "I don't know. He does have a bad temper and didn't like the mayor. But this thing is wide open right now. I think there were probably a lot of people that didn't like our illustrious former mayor, but that's not reason enough to suspect all of them."

"I hope he didn't. I'd hate to see someone that really wants the town to succeed go to jail," I said.

"Like I said, it could be anyone at this point."

"Oh, I almost forgot. I overheard Susan Goodall and Jerry Crownover arguing. It sounded suspicious. They were each accusing each other of doing something."

"Doing what?" he asked.

I shrugged, suddenly feeling silly. "I don't know exactly. But Susan said if he had thought something out, it would have gone smoother. Only, I didn't hear everything they were saying so I don't have details. Sorry. But I really feel like it had something to do with the murder."

Ethan laughed. "Well, I'll keep it in mind. You never know."

I knew he thought I was being ridiculous, but the more I thought about it, the more I thought it might have something to do with the murder. I wished I had been quieter when I walked up behind them. I needed to work on my sneaking skills.

Amanda and Brian sidled up to us.

"Hi, Brian. Hi Amanda," I said.

"Hey, guys. Good to see you both here."

"Andrea's really good," Amanda said. "I'm jealous."

"Me too. It's hard to believe all of that is natural talent," I said. "She's wasting her time staying in this town."

Andrea finished up her set and headed over to us. Her eyes were shining as people applauded.

"You were great, Andrea," Ethan said above the noise.

"You are so fantastic," Amanda said and gave Andrea a hug. "We've decided we're jealous of you."

"I loved it," I told her. Andrea blushed under the praise and it made her look even more beautiful.

"Thanks guys," she said. "You guys are so sweet."

"When are you going to make a break for it and head to L.A. or New York?" Brian asked. "You could have a great career."

I nodded. Andrea had more than a great voice. She had a great stage presence.

"I don't know. That's kind of scary," Andrea said. She held onto a charm on a chain around her neck and moved it back and forth.

"But you could do it," I said. "At the very least, you should audition for one of those television talent searches."

"I might take your advice about trying out for one of the TV shows. I don't know if I'll do it though. I've got school. My dad is on me all the time about getting good grades so I can get a scholarship and maybe get into a university. I've got to have a scholarship or we won't be able to afford the tuition. At least I'll have my AA degree when I finish at the junior college and that'll save some money."

"What are you studying?" Brian asked.

"Well, I wanted to go to med school, but I didn't get a scholarship to go to a university, so I don't know if I can get into one now or not," Andrea said, frowning. "I would have gotten a scholarship, you know, except that–" And she stopped.

"Except what?" I asked. College was expensive and her parents weren't wealthy.

"Except that the money the glee club raised when I was in high school suddenly disappeared," she said bitterly. "If we'd been able to compete for those scholarships at regionals, I would have had the money to go to a university. I'm sure I would have won. Now I'm stuck going to a junior college."

"That was a real shame," Amanda said, nodding her blond head.

"Didn't the school look into it?" Ethan asked thoughtfully.

"Oh, sure. If you want to call it that. But they didn't do anything to him and we didn't get to go to the competition. So here I am, still stuck in Pumpkin Hollow, going to junior college." Her face went red as she spoke and she gripped the charm on her necklace.

"That's a shame," Ethan said. "I would have thought they would have looked into it more closely."

"Wouldn't you think so?" Andrea asked bitterly. "It made no sense. The school just didn't care."

"I think if you get really good grades and get into a university, you shouldn't have a problem getting into med school," Amanda said. "It stinks that you have to take the long way around, but if you really want this, I think things will work out."

Andrea looked up at her, opened her mouth to say something, and then closed it for a moment. Tears sprang to her eyes and she blinked them away. "You're right. I'm sure things will work out. Things are the way they are for a reason and everything will work out."

"Right," I said and put my hand on her arm and gave it a squeeze. "Sometimes the long way around is what we're meant to take to keep us from harm."

She nodded. "It will be fine," she said and forced herself to smile. "Everything will be fine."

There was loud laughter from the bar and we all turned to look.

Fagan was holding up a shot glass filled with amber liquid. "A toast to the death of the biggest hindrance to Pumpkin Hollow's success."

Chapter Fourteen

"What do you have that's pumpkin spice flavored?" I heard a voice say. I was sitting on the floor behind the counter during a slow moment, wiping the crevices of the display case. The case was over eighty years old and there were lots of grooves and crevices carved into the wood base. I had somehow missed the sound of the bell on the door signaling a customer had entered the store.

I jumped to my feet and popped up from behind the counter. "Hi, Mrs. Goodall," I said. "We have pumpkin fudge and pumpkin truffles. I'm sure we'll come up with other items as the season goes on."

"Fudge. I want some fudge," she said, pointing to the fudge in the display case. I had just made a fresh batch less than an hour earlier.

"Great, how much would you like?" I could smell a hint of alcohol on her breath and her finger trembled when she pointed.

"All of it," she said. "I love pumpkin fudge. I love pumpkin everything."

"That's about three pounds," I said. "Are you sure?"

"Yes," she said, and swayed on her feet. "I like it. You should sell pumpkin spice lattes. It would bring more business in here."

"Okay, then, let me wrap that up," I said, ignoring her advice on the lattes. She didn't seem to be herself and I hoped she didn't regret buying all that fudge.

I went to the display case and opened it. It was only 10:30 in the morning, but she seemed a bit drunk.

"How have you been, Mrs. Goodall?" I asked.

"I've never felt this bad. I lost the love of my life. Why would someone do that to him?" Her voice cracked as she spoke and I thought for a minute she might break down.

"I don't know how anyone can take another's life," I said. "I'm so sorry."

"I'll tell you, this whole Halloween thing is a menace. Bad things happen. There's a curse on this town. Have you heard about it? A curse!"

I bit my lower lip. I didn't want to argue with her in her state. "I'm sorry," I said.

"I know who did it," she said, swaying on her feet.

"Oh? Who would that be?" I asked, cutting the fudge into more manageable pieces. The more she talked, the more I realized she really was drunk. I felt like it might have been a little unconscionable that I was letting her buy three pounds of fudge. It was expensive.

She nodded her head and put both hands on the counter in front of her to steady herself. "Yes. It's that Fagan Branigan. Jerry told me how much Fagan hated Stan. Fagan was against him. He wants to keep the Halloween season."

"Mrs. Goodall, there are a lot of people that want to keep the Halloween season," I pointed out. Her reasoning didn't seem sound.

She breathed out deeply and I got another whiff of alcohol. "Listen, he told my husband he would stop him no matter what. Well, that's exactly what he did. He stopped him." She broke down crying then. "And he's getting away with it!"

"I'm sorry," I said, and wrapped up the fudge. "Did you talk to the police about what your husband told you?" Fagan's name hadn't come up when Ethan and I spoke to her after Stan's death.

"Of course I did. They didn't think much of it or he would be in jail by now," she said, waving a hand at me.

I reached under the counter and picked up the box of tissues and handed them to her. She grabbed three out and blew her nose into them.

"You know how the police are. It takes them time to gather evidence. I'm sure they'll arrest the killer soon. Whoever it is," I assured her.

"Sure they will," she said angrily. "You know, I don't know why Stan stayed in this town. It's too small and narrow-minded. He had ideas and dreams. He was too good for this place. No one appreciated him!"

"He was the mayor. I'm sure he did a lot of good for the town. I haven't been back long, but I'm sure he did a lot," I said, trying to reassure her that he was appreciated.

She snorted. "He was lazy. I told him dreams don't count for much unless you act on them. I know if he had lived, I would have gotten him to act on them. I would have made him act on them. But he was lazy. There, I said it. No one else is in here, right?" she said and looked around, almost falling over with the effort. She steadied herself against the front counter. "He was lazy. He infuriated me. I thought I married a get-it-done man. A man that had ambition. It's a shame, really. So much wasted potential."

I stared at her. First he was the best thing that happened to her and the town, and then he was too lazy to do anything.

She was obviously too drunk to drive. She couldn't even get her thoughts straight. "Mrs. Goodall, you didn't drive here, did you?" I asked.

"Well, I didn't ride in on a broom," she said. "That idiot husband of mine was a waste of time."

This conversation was making me terribly uncomfortable. "Maybe I can give you a ride home," I offered. I didn't think Mrs. Goodall should drive in her condition. My mother and Andrea were in the kitchen and if I could get Mrs. Goodall to hand over her keys, I would take her home.

"Nonsense. I drove over here, didn't I?" she said.

I rang up her fudge, trying to come up with a way to convince her not to drive.

"I think it would be a good idea for me to drive you home," I insisted. "Have you been drinking?"

"I had a beer. It's not like I'm drunk," she insisted as she tried to get her debit card into the card reader. Her hand shook and each time she tried to get the card in the slot, she missed.

"Would you like some help with that?" I asked and took the card from her.

"Yes, fine," she said. "But I haven't had that much to drink."

I ran the card through as a credit card. Her hitting the right numbers on the keypad to use it as a debit card wasn't going to happen. When the sale went through, I looked at her and smiled.

"Mrs. Goodall, why don't you give me your keys and I'll drive you home?"

She shook her head. "I'm not drunk. I'm going to drive myself." She reached over and picked up the bag of fudge.

"Really, Mrs. Goodall, I'm going to ask you for your keys again," I said calmly. "Otherwise I'll call the police."

She looked at me and narrowed her eyes. "I used to think you were a nice person. My husband was killed and it was one of your friends that killed him. You're a terrible person, Mia Jordan."

"Fagan isn't a friend, he's another merchant, and the police haven't yet determined who killed your husband. I want to do you a favor and keep you from hurting yourself," I said, trying to remain calm.

"I am not drunk!" she insisted. "Don't say that about me! You're a gossip!"

I sighed and handed her debit card back to her. "Do I give you a ride home, or do I call the police?"

She glared at me. "Fine. Drive me home."

SUSAN RANTED AND RAVED about her husband's death while I drove her home. I tried not to take it personally, but she wasn't the nicest person when she was drinking. I reminded myself that her husband had died and she didn't mean anything she said.

After seeing her safely into her house, I pulled my phone out of my pocket and called Ethan to ask for a ride back to the shop.

"That's a good thing you did," he said when I got into the car.

I sighed. "I couldn't have her hurting herself or someone else. She thinks Fagan killed the mayor."

"At this point, things are kind of pointing in that direction," he said. "Mum's the word on that, though."

"How is it pointing to him? Besides his general dislike of the mayor?"

"There were a large number of boot prints at the corn maze. All made by the same boot. On the day of the fire, Fagan was wearing boots that made prints that matched the prints found around the maze. Fagan admitted they matched but he said he had been there looking at the maze," Ethan said with a shrug. "He went downtown and he was interviewed. He backtracked on some statements he made earlier. But there still isn't enough evidence to make an arrest."

"But there have been a lot of people in and around the mazes. They could have been made by anyone, and not necessarily the killer," I pointed out.

"That's true, but they were also in the area where the mayor was found, and not many people had been back there because they didn't put any actors or lights down that aisle," he said. "The boot prints may not have been made by the killer, and boot prints are thin evidence, but backtracking on statements raises suspicions."

I laid my head back against the seat and stared up at the top of the squad car. "I hope it's not him. But if it is, I hope he's arrested soon so we can put this behind us."

"Will you go out with me to dinner? Someplace we can talk without lots of music and other people?" Ethan asked.

"We can't go somewhere there are other people?" I asked. "Do you want to go someplace deserted?"

He smiled. "You know what I mean."

I turned to him and smiled. "Okay."

Chapter Fifteen

I agreed to go to dinner with Ethan at the barbecue place in town. Not that I had to be talked into it. I found Ethan was on my mind more and more lately. Sometimes I didn't hear something someone said because I was thinking so hard about him. Three days ago I gave a customer two pounds of taffy instead of a pound of taffy and a pound of bonbons.

Going out with Ethan was going to be easy. But there were some questions I had. Like, did I want to go out with someone that got paid to be shot at? I wasn't sure. I took a deep breath and looked at myself in the mirror. I was wearing jeans and a cute blue top that set off the color of my eyes. I reminded myself that there was no reason to think about a future with Ethan yet. We'd only had one date. I liked him and he liked me and that was enough for now.

THE HOSTESS LED US to a table in the back and I slid into the booth. The Pumpkin Hollow Barbecue Shack was a fun, casual place with crushed peanut shells on the floor and an antique jukebox in the corner that played alternating country music and good ol' boy rock and roll.

"What can I get you to drink?" the hostess asked.

"Iced tea," I said.

"I'll have the same," Ethan said.

"I'll be right back with," she said and slid two menus onto the table.

"So, how are you this evening?" Ethan asked, slipping into the seat across from me.

"I'm great. I'm also starving," I said, opening the menu the hostess left. "Do you know what you're going to have?"

"Baby back ribs. They're the best in the county," he said, not bothering to open the menu. He wore a blue plaid button down shirt and jeans and was as handsome as could be. It amazed me that he managed to look so different when out of uniform.

"That sounds good. I think I'll have the pulled pork sandwich."

"A fine choice," he said. "How's business at the candy store?"

"Not bad. Fortunately for us, candy is popular all year long, but especially this time of year," I said. "Anything new on the mayor's death?"

He shook his head. "They're processing the bullets, but matching them up to the murder weapon and tracing who a gun belongs to isn't as easy as they make it seem on TV. That will take some time."

I nodded. Patience wasn't my strong suit. I wanted answers and I wanted to put this murder business behind us.

"Susan Goodall was kind of odd yesterday," I said. "I know she was drunk, but at first she was talking like her husband Stan was so talented and was too good for the town, then she went on to say he was lazy and wouldn't do anything without her there to force him."

He grinned. "Alcohol is a crazy maker. Maybe they were having marital problems before he died and she's having a problem getting over it. It can't be easy, having your husband killed."

"I know. I guess I'm not being nice," I said.

The waitress brought us our iced tea and took our orders. The smell of hickory-smoked barbecue in the air made my stomach growl and I hoped they brought our food out fast.

"Here's something I'm wondering," he said, taking a sip of his iced tea, then putting the glass down on the table. "Why were you at college for ten years?"

I looked at him, and then looked at my glass. It still embarrassed me that I had spent so many years in school and came back to work in my parents' candy shop. I had received lots of scholarship money and worked the whole time I was in school, but it still left me with loans to pay back.

"I guess you could say I had trouble making up my mind about what I want to do with my life," I said, and tried to smile to hide the embarrassment. "I did end up with a couple of master's degrees, so I feel I'm well prepared for whatever life throws my way."

"What kind of degrees?" he asked. "I know you told me about business and web development."

"Well, I started out thinking I would become a veterinarian, but the sight of blood and dissected critters really bothered me, so I switched to English Literature. I was sure I wanted to either write or teach at the local junior college. But then I had second thoughts and I got a master's in business and web development. How does that sound?"

He nodded. "Sounds like you're prepared for life."

"Except now I'm right back where I started. I could have gone to work in my parents' candy store from the start and not gotten myself so deep in debt with college loans."

"I wouldn't sweat it. I bet those degrees come in handy at some point. You've already used your master's in web development. Something will turn up for you."

I smiled. Ethan was an awesome guy. He had turned something I felt so embarrassed about into something that sounded positive. "Thanks. I hope it does. What about you? I always thought you would be a lawyer or something."

He shrugged. "Like I said before, my parents sure thought I was going to go to college and do something big. But here I am, protecting and serving the good people of Pumpkin Hollow."

"I think law enforcement is a noble profession," I said, taking a sip of my iced tea.

He laughed. "Thanks, I never thought of it as noble."

"Well, it is. I'm glad you did something you wanted and not something your parents wanted you to do."

"Were you seeing someone in Michigan?" he asked abruptly.

"No one serious. There were a couple of relationships that were good, but things didn't work out. Sometimes I think I'm the most boring girlfriend in the world. My relationships always end on good terms. No thrown vases of flowers and no bitterness. Well, maybe a little bitterness, but nothing bad enough to cause me to stalk anyone."

"That's a great way to end a relationship," he said. "Stalking is overrated."

I shrugged. "I was never one for drama. I don't put anything on social media, so there's nothing to bitterly complain about when it's over. Tell me what it's like being a small town policeman."

"Not bad. I don't get shot at as frequently as big town police officers do, but we have our share of drugs and thefts. And recently, murders."

I smiled at him. I was glad we didn't live in a larger city where there was a greater chance he might get shot.

"Don't tell me what to do!"

We both looked toward the front of the restaurant where Susan Goodall was being guided toward the front door by what looked like a couple of busboys.

"I know my rights. We'll stop this whole Halloween thing if it's the last thing we do!" Susan shouted, slurring her words. She had on a short black skirt and a blouse that was cut lower than it should be. It reminded me of the outfits she used to wear when I was in school.

I looked at Ethan, and he raised his eyebrows at me.

"I swear, we will end this Halloween season!" Susan cried. The two busboys had their hands full trying to usher her toward the door, but she broke free of them and ran to the middle of the restaurant. "I know who murdered my husband! I want justice!"

Ethan sighed. "Excuse me a minute."

Ethan got up and walked slowly toward her. When he got to her, I could just hear him telling her to calm down.

"I am calm!" she insisted. She was still speaking loudly, but had stopped shouting. "I need justice."

"I understand," Ethan said. "But you can't act like this in public. Can I call someone to pick you up?"

"I don't need anyone to pick me up," she said, straightening her blouse.

"Let's go outside and talk," he said. Susan went with him willingly. There were whispers and a low-key laughter throughout the restaurant. They were outside for ten minutes before Ethan came back in alone.

He smiled as he sat across from me. "Sorry," he said.

"Don't be. It's good you were here to keep her from driving. This is the second time she's been drunk in public and it makes me think she has a real drinking problem."

"She's insisting Fagan killed her husband and as retribution she's going to make sure the vote to stop the Halloween season passes. Or she'll burn the town down."

I gasped. "She didn't say that, did she?"

"She did. I warned her that if she kept making threats she was going to have to take a ride downtown."

"Wow," I said. "She needs help."

"I told her that, too. In light of the recent fire, she shouldn't say things like that," he said.

"Do you think she had something to do with that fire?" I whispered. I didn't want anyone to overhear a question like that.

"I don't think so. We needed to go over that field one more time for evidence in her husband's death and the fire destroyed anything left behind. I don't think she would have done that."

"But if the fire cast a blight on the town's reputation, she might have done it to get rid of the Halloween season," I pointed out. "Maybe she killed Stan and set the fire to cover up evidence."

He thought about it a moment. "Anything's possible, but I don't think so. I think she's just an angry, hurt woman that's trying to ease her pain with alcohol. Maybe I should have become a therapist."

I snorted. "Isn't that what you are? I would think you hear an awful lot as a police officer."

He nodded. "You've got a point. I've heard more sad stories than most therapists do, I think. I would have been paid better as a therapist. I may have made a grave mistake in my choice of career."

I laughed. "You may have."

The waitress brought our food and my stomach growled.

"That smells so good," I said. It was nearly fall and something about barbecue and the cold fall weather went together. We would have to do this again when it got colder. For now, I would enjoy Ethan's company. I might also pretend Pumpkin Hollow didn't have a killer on the loose and while I was at it, I might as well pretend there wasn't going to be a vote to determine whether we got to keep our Halloween celebration.

Chapter Sixteen

On Monday evening, I was sitting beside Ethan at the town council meeting. It would be the final meeting before the special vote was taken and everyone would have a chance to express their opinions on whether we should keep the Halloween theme or go back to being a plain, ordinary small town.

At the front desk sat council member Tracy Goode, filling in for the now deceased mayor until someone was sworn in as permanent mayor. I didn't know Tracy and I wondered if she was pro Halloween season.

"Ladies and gentlemen," Tracy began. "We'd all like to observe a moment of silence at the passing of our honorable Mayor, Stan Goodall. Let's bow our heads."

I put my head down, but peeked. I could see people around me that didn't have the courtesy to bow their heads. I sighed. Even if they couldn't stand the guy, he was a person and someone had killed him. They could have just bowed their head and pretended to be respectful.

"Now, let's get on with business," Tracy said. "There's a motion to end the Halloween season. Would anyone like to speak?"

I was surprised she went straight to letting people speak. I had thought she would monopolize the meeting with her own opinions. Fagan stood up, along with a couple of other people.

"Vincent Moretti, would you like to get us started?" Tracy said, looking past Fagan.

"Yes, I would," Vincent said. "It's high time we stopped this Halloween season. It costs us more than it gives back. My wife has all kinds of ideas about changing our business, but she can't because of the Halloween theme. If we got rid of it, she could make the changes and we'd make more money, and thereby bring in more tax money for the town."

Tracy made a note. "That's a wonderful observation," she said. "We're all about businesses prospering and in turn, the town prospering."

I rolled my eyes and looked at Ethan. He shook his head.

"Who's next?" Tracy asked.

Fagan jumped to his feet again, but Tracy called on Jessie Sterling.

"We need to end the Halloween season because it brings in more crime," Jesse pointed out. "When we have lots of tourists, things get stolen. Everyone knows you have to lock things up during the Halloween season and I'm tired of it. I have a right to have a safe city to live in. Not to mention a couple of murders now. It's all because of the Halloween season."

I looked at Ethan. Was it true there was more crime during the Halloween season? He gave me a look that said it was true. I slouched down in my seat. I had never considered it, but I guess it made sense. Tourists were strangers to town and the Halloween season drew people from all walks of life. But I couldn't imagine the increase in crime could be that great.

I sat back and listened to everyone giving their views. The longer the meeting went on, the more I felt we were going to lose. They must have spent at least a week rounding up nearly everyone in town that didn't like the Halloween season. I took a deep breath and as one of the other business owners was wrapping up their views in support of Halloween, got ready to get to my feet.

Fagan jumped up ahead of me. "I'm going to speak now, whether you like it or not," he said to Tracy. "We merchants in Pumpkin Hollow are hard workers. We're all just trying to make a living. We have families and we have dreams. You have no right to take those dreams from us. This nonsense about the Halloween season bringing more crime to town is just that. Nonsense. Every town has crime and Pumpkin Hollow is no different. Blaming it on the Halloween season is ludicrous." Fagan sat down, folding his arms across his chest.

"Thank you, Fagan. Your opinion has been noted," Tracy said with a sigh. "Now that we've heard everyone's opinions and views on this subject, we'll put it to a vote of the city council members."

What?

I jumped to my feet. "Wait a minute," I said. "Mayor Goodall said we would take a vote. Business owners and community members alike would vote. No one said city council members would vote."

"You don't have the floor," Tracy said. "Sit down."

"No, I will not sit down! We have a right to vote!"

Tracy sighed loudly. "The former Mayor Goodall made a mistake. Council members will vote on the ordinance."

"That's not right. We have a right to vote on our future and we were told we could do that," I said. "We have rights!"

"That's right," Fagan said, jumping to his feet. "You can't just change the rules at the last minute."

I could hear a murmur rising in the room and I hoped it was people standing behind the Halloween season. I looked at Ethan and he gave me a thumbs up.

"Quiet!" Tracy said and slammed a gavel on the desk. "I'll have people removed!"

I narrowed my eyes at Tracy. We might have ended up with a worse situation than before Stan was murdered. At least with Stan around, we had a chance at a vote.

A man in a suit that I recognized but didn't know got up and went to Tracy. He leaned over and whispered in her ear and she nodded. They spoke to one another for a few moments before the man turned and went back to his seat.

"We're going to put this off while we investigate the city laws regarding passing ordinances," Tracy said and pounded the table with the gavel again. She got to her feet and went out a side door before anyone could say anything else.

I got to my feet and glared at the door Tracy had left by.

Ethan stood up and put an arm around my shoulders. "You did great."

"I don't know if I did. What's going on here?" I asked him. "We're supposed to vote. I didn't get a chance to tell my part."

"Smoke and mirrors," he said. "If you ask me, they're trying to drag this thing out. But let's just look on it as us having more time to change things and get people to vote with us."

"If we get to vote, you mean," I said and we moved down the aisle of seats.

"We're going to get to vote," Fagan said as we stepped out into the aisle. "We aren't going to be railroaded by another corrupt politician. You wait and see."

"I hope so," I said.

"We got this," Dan Jefferson said as we headed toward the door. "We're going to get it done." Dan owned a café in the Halloween district and was on our side.

I nodded and reached behind me for Ethan's hand. Out front of the courthouse several people stood around and talked.

"We need to get rid of the Halloween season," Joe Smithson said. "It's an annoyance and I'm tired of paying high taxes to support it." Joe was a citizen in the community and was known for being a loudmouth. He was someone I usually tried to avoid.

"Come on Joe, no one is taxed as high as the Halloween businesses. That's a myth that regular people are taxed higher because of the Halloween season," I said. "I'm tired of people complaining about things that have nothing to do with them."

"Look at you, you haven't even been back in town for a month. You don't even know what's going on around here," Joe said. He stuck his chest out and got in my face, trying to stare me down.

"I'd be taking a few steps back, Joe," Ethan said quietly.

He looked over at Ethan, and then backed up two steps. He looked at me. "I don't mean anything by it, I just don't think we should pay for this silly stuff."

"Well, you aren't," I said. "We need to pull together for this town. It's more than just keeping the business district going. It's about our heritage, and our livelihoods. If our businesses suffer, they all suffer. If businesses close, then people do without or have to drive more than thirty miles to buy what they need. Then people start moving away because it's more convenient to live in a town where they have what people need. And that just leads to the demise of the town."

Joe continued staring at me a moment longer. "I got to get home," he said and turned around and left.

I looked at Ethan as people started wandering away.

"Chin up," Fagan said. "We'll be fine. Stan couldn't stop us, and neither is anyone else. Just watch and see."

We watched as Fagan walked across the parking lot and got into his pickup truck.

"Makes you wonder if he stopped Stan, doesn't it?" I whispered to Ethan.

"It does. But then, a lot of people make me wonder whether they stopped Stan," he said.

"Me, too," I said and we followed the last of the people out to the parking lot.

I couldn't help feeling like we had lost a round.

Chapter Seventeen

I had done it. I made two-dozen chocolate cupcakes and swirled orange frosting on top. Spun sugar adorned the tops of some, while others had orange marzipan pumpkins and bats. They looked wonderful and I couldn't resist trying one out before putting them in the display case. I was not disappointed. I put them on a tray while I finished up with some candy before taking them out to the display case.

I was pouring milk chocolate into molds to make jack-o-lantern candies when I heard the bell over the front door. Mom wasn't feeling well and I was working the morning shift alone. Andrea would be here in fifteen minutes and Lisa would work the afternoon shift when she got out of school. I laid the silicone spatula down and wiped my hands on my apron.

"Coming!" I called, took the apron off and tossed it onto a counter, and headed for the shop floor.

Stella Moretti was leaning over, looking at the candy in the display case. She looked up at me and narrowed her eyes. "I was expecting your mother to be here."

I gave her a smile, and was glad I hadn't yet brought the cupcakes out to the display case. Mom was right. Stella would have a fit when she saw them, but she was the one that resisted fully participating in the Halloween season, so she had no one to blame but herself.

"She wasn't feeling well, so I told her to stay home. How are you, Stella?"

"I'm fine," she said. She returned her attention to the display case, but then gave me a little side-eye.

"I just made a fresh batch of pumpkin fudge," I offered. "I know you like the pumpkin fudge."

She straightened up. "I love the pumpkin fudge. In fact, I love all the candy your mother makes."

There was an emphasis on "your mother". I kept smiling though. Stella was a grump sometimes and I wasn't going to let her ruin my day.

"Mom does make some great candy," I agreed. "She learned from her mother and I've had the privilege of learning from my mother."

"You know something, Mia?" she asked. "My husband, Vince, saw Fagan Branigan at the bar last night."

"Oh," I said. "That's nice." Vince could drink with the best of them, and I preferred to keep my distance from him when he did. He was a nice guy, but he got loud and sloppy when he drank.

"You know what he said?" she asked, waiting.

"Um, Vince, or Fagan?" I asked, and sat down on the stool behind the front counter.

"Fagan. He told Vince he was glad Stan Goodall was dead. He also said he wished everyone that opposed the Halloween season would meet the same fate." She put her hands on her ample hips and stared at me.

"Well, a lot of people aren't grieving for the mayor, and I guess everyone has a right to their opinion about the Halloween season," I said, ignoring the part where he wished everyone supporting ending the Halloween season should meet the same fate. "Personally, I think it's a terrible tragedy when someone is murdered."

I wasn't sure why she was telling me this and why she seemed angry with me.

"He also said that if the new mayor opposed the Halloween season, they might meet the same fate Stan did. That sounds like a threat, to me," she said. "I think the police should be informed of this."

"Well, since the conversation took place in a bar, I'd be willing to bet alcohol had some influence on what he was saying. In fact, I bet alcohol influenced a whole lot of the things being said in the bar last night."

I glanced at the cuckoo clock on the far wall and wished the little headless horseman would pop out, signaling 11:00 and time for Andrea to show up. I wasn't sure what Stella's problem was, but it felt like she thought I had something to do with this situation.

"You know what, Mia Jordan? I think you are the cause of the trouble around here."

"Wait, what?" I asked. "That doesn't make sense."

"You come back here with your big ideas and you decide everyone has to believe in the Halloween season like you do. Then everyone gets mad at each other because some want the season to end and others want it to continue and then people start dying. I'd say that's pretty suspicious, if you ask me," she glowered.

"Now wait a minute. I had nothing to do with either murder. It had nothing to do with me and I wasn't the one that decided to stop the Halloween season. That was Stan Goodall and Jerry Crownover. I don't know what you're talking about."

"You may not have killed either Hazel Martin or Stan Goodall with your own hands, but you killed them just the same by stirring people up and getting them angry. You little do-gooder, you!"

I gasped. "Stella, you're going too far. I had nothing to do with either murder. I had nothing to do with even putting this measure up for vote. Honestly, Stella, I think you're out of your mind. And if Fagan really did sound like he was threatening someone, then Vince needs to report it to the police so they can look into it." I didn't know where all this hostility was coming from. I couldn't smell any alcohol on Stella's breath, so it couldn't be that, but things were getting crazy.

She narrowed her eyes at me. "You had better keep your mouth shut, Mia Jordan. You're stirring up trouble and you know you are. Stop before you get someone else killed."

"Stella! I don't know why you're saying these things. You know I had nothing to do with the murders!" I said louder than I meant to, and I slipped down off the stool. I went to the front counter and leaned on it. "I don't know where this is coming from."

She breathed out hard. "Mia, just leave things alone. We don't need another murder. There's a curse on this town. But maybe the curse is really just someone stirring up trouble."

She turned around and walked out, leaving me standing there with my mouth open. How could she even think I had influenced someone to murder, or stirred up trouble of any kind?

Andrea pushed the door open two minutes later and I was still standing at the counter, trying to get my thoughts together.

"Hi Mia, how are you today?" she asked. She looked at me and stopped in her tracks. "Mia, are you okay?"

I opened my mouth and then closed it. I could feel tears welling up, but I blinked them back. I forced myself to smile. "I'm fine, Andrea. Just fine. How are you?"

"You don't look fine," she said, shaking her head.

"Between you and me, Stella Moretti was just in here and she said I was stirring up trouble by trying to save the Halloween season."

"Are you serious?" she asked, wide-eyed. "What does she mean, stirring up trouble?"

"I guess anyone that doesn't want what she wants is a troublemaker. She said it was my fault Hazel and the mayor were murdered." The absurdity of it was stunning and I wasn't sure what to do about it.

"That's just crazy," she said, and came around behind the counter with me. "You don't think she'll tell other people that, do you?"

I stared at her. It hadn't occurred to me that she would spread it around, but of course she would. Stella wasn't a shy wallflower where her opinion was concerned. She'd tell it and she'd tell everyone. My heart dropped. How do you stop the rumor mill?

"I'm sure she will," I said and picked up a cloth and started cleaning the front counter. Cleaning was what I did when I didn't want to think about something.

"I'm sorry, Mia, I shouldn't have said that. Everyone knows you had nothing to do with those murders."

Andrea stowed her purse under the front counter. "So, have you heard anything new about the mayor's murder? Do they have suspects?"

"I haven't heard that they have. I'm sure they'll find the killer," I said.

"Do you think they will with the burned corn maze? It seems like that would have destroyed the evidence if the police didn't find it all," she said, picking up some business cards and shuffling them in her hand.

"I don't know. Sometimes things don't completely burn up in a fire like people think they do. I saw a show on it once. Anyway, criminals usually give themselves away," I said. "I have complete confidence in the police department to find the mayor's killer."

"What do you mean?" she asked and dropped the business cards. She bent down and picked them up.

"You see it all the time. Criminals over-think everything and give themselves away. Ever watch one of those true crime shows?" I asked.

"Um, sure, I've seen a few, I guess," she said quietly.

I looked at her. Her hands were trembling as she put the business cards back into the holder on the front counter.

"How are you doing, Andrea?" I asked.

"I'm great. I've got three tests tomorrow and I haven't even studied yet. I'm a little worried about failing, but I'm probably worrying over nothing."

"I'm sure you'll do fine. You're a smart cookie," I said. "Well, I was making chocolate jack-o-lanterns in the kitchen and I'm sure the chocolate has hardened by now. I'm going to start over. Watch the front for me?"

"Sure," she said with a stiff smile. "I'll keep an eye on things."

I headed to the back and hoped Stella would keep her mouth shut for once. The chances that she would were slim to none, but I wasn't going to worry about it right then.

Chapter Eighteen

The more I thought about what Stella had said, the angrier I became. Where did she get off saying that I was the cause of the murders? And why did Fagan have to go around telling everyone he was glad the mayor had died? If he had any sense in that big noggin of his, he would just keep his mouth shut. It wasn't any secret that Fagan was happy about the mayor being dead. All his talk did was stir up trouble and we would all be better off if he would keep quiet.

When things had slowed down at the store, I decided to take a walk over to the costume shop and see Fagan myself. I wasn't sure I could talk him into keeping his mouth shut, but I was going to try. If he didn't, the police might decide the boot prints were enough to try him for murder.

I stepped out onto the sidewalk, letting the candy shop door close quietly behind me. I looked in the direction of the costume shop and saw two police cars parked in front. I gasped, wondering what was going on, and hurried over to the shop. Fagan's mouth might have gotten him in trouble after all.

I hoped it was Ethan at the costume shop, but when I got closer, I saw that neither squad car was his. I pushed the shop door open and went inside, not caring that the police were there.

It was as bad as I had feared. A police officer was putting handcuffs on Fagan. Fagan looked up at me and gave me a hard look. I would have sworn that Fagan could not have killed the mayor, but now I wondered if I was wrong.

"You're making a mistake," Samantha Branigan said. Samantha was Fagan's wife and she stood behind the counter with tears streaming down her face.

It broke my heart for her to see her husband being arrested. Samantha was a sweet woman, and was Fagan's complete opposite.

"Tell your boyfriend I didn't kill anyone," Fagan said bitterly to me. His face was red and he huffed when he spoke.

"Fagan, I'm sure there's been some kind of a mistake," I said. "We'll get to the bottom of this."

"You better believe we'll get to the bottom of this," he said. "Samantha, call a lawyer."

"I will," she sobbed. "This is a mistake."

I stood and watched as the police took Fagan from the store and put him into the back of the police car. I looked over at Samantha, and she put her hand to her mouth and looked at me wide-eyed.

"I'm sure it will be okay, Samantha," I said. "Everyone knows Fagan wouldn't kill the mayor." Except that he had told nearly everyone in town that he was glad the mayor was dead. That part worried me. Someone had talked to the police and told them what Fagan was saying.

"I can't believe they're doing this," Samantha said. "This is ridiculous. Fagan would never do something like this."

"I'm sure there's been a mistake," I said. I bit my lip to keep from saying Fagan should have kept his mouth shut. That was the last thing she needed to hear.

I went out onto the sidewalk and texted Ethan, asking him to meet me here at the costume shop. I was sure he had heard about Fagan's arrest and while I wasn't sure if he could tell me much, I was going to ask him anyway.

Five minutes later, a police car pulled up to the curb and I could see Ethan behind the wheel. I went to the driver's side door and he opened it and got out of the car.

"They just took Fagan away in handcuffs," I informed him.

"I know. I heard the call. I was on another call so I couldn't get here," Ethan said.

"I keep going back and forth in my mind as to whether Fagan murdered the mayor," I said. "He has a big mouth and he likes to talk a lot, but I don't know if he would actually kill him. What do you think?"

"Mia, he was running all over town, telling everyone he was glad the mayor was dead," Ethan said, putting his hands on my shoulders and looking me in the eye.

"But that isn't enough to arrest someone," I pointed out. "I don't think boot prints are, either."

"They wouldn't have made an arrest without evidence," he said. "If Fagan is innocent, he doesn't act like it."

He was right. I just didn't want to believe it. I looked into his eyes. "Stella Moretti was just in my shop. She said Fagan was at the bar bragging and telling everyone that he was glad the mayor had been murdered. Why would he do something stupid like that? People are going to blame him just because he can't shut his mouth."

Ethan sighed. "Some people don't have any common sense. He better have a good alibi."

"She also said the murders were my fault because I was stirring up trouble over the Halloween season." My voice cracked when I said it and I silently cursed myself.

"Mia, that's idiocy. Don't let her get to you. You know you had nothing to do with any of this."

Relief flowed over me. I needed to hear him say the words, even though I already knew the truth. He pulled me to him and held me close.

"Did the police know he was telling everyone he was glad about the murder?" I asked, leaning against his chest.

"Of course. Pumpkin Hollow is a small town and Fagan has a big mouth," Ethan said, letting me go. "I broke up a fight between him and Vince Moretti last night at the bar. Fagan's been getting himself into trouble. He shouldn't have been surprised about being arrested."

"You're right. I shouldn't get upset over what Stella said."

"That's right. Her opinion doesn't mean a thing," he said. "We borrowed a detective from another department and he's been working on the case. We'll have the facts soon and you can tell Stella to shut her mouth. She's just a busybody anyway."

"Was Fagan somebody that was a suspect early on in the case?" I asked.

He nodded. "But that's confidential information," he said. "They aren't releasing the names of any of the people they've been interviewing. I can tell you there have been several people of interest. But again, that's confidential and we need to keep it quiet."

"Got it. I won't tell anybody. I just hope they find the killer. Did they get back any information from the autopsy?"

"Six .45 ACP bullets were recovered from his body. It's a very common bullet and there's nothing surprising about it."

"He was shot six times? It sounds like overkill, no pun intended," I said.

"There could have been a little passion behind it, or maybe the killer just wanted to make sure he didn't get up and walk away," he said with a shrug. "They're still looking at other evidence they found in the corn maze."

The door to the costume shop swung open and Samantha stood there with tears in her eyes. She closed the door behind her and locked it. Then she turned around and looked at Ethan.

"Did you hear Fagan was arrested?" she asked Ethan. "He had nothing to do with the death of the mayor. There is no reason for him to be arrested!"

"I'm sorry, Samantha," Ethan said. "I heard there was an arrest warrant called in by dispatch."

"I told Fagan not to go around telling people he was glad the mayor was dead. He said he had nothing to lose because he didn't have anything to do with the murder. I told him people are falsely arrested all the time. I don't know what's wrong with that man. I told him and told him to keep his mouth shut."

Ethan's mouth made a straight line. "I'm sorry you're going through this, Samantha. I recommend getting a lawyer as soon as possible."

"I will. I've got to go now," she said.

We watched as Samantha got into her car and drove away.

"I sure hope the police figure out what's going on around here. I'm trying not to believe there's a curse, but Pumpkin Hollow has changed so much since I was a kid."

"We're doing our best," he said.

I knew he was right. The police would figure out who killed the mayor, whether it was Fagan or not, and things would get back to normal. I hoped.

Chapter Nineteen

I pushed open the coffee shop door and entered. Amanda was behind the counter making a coffee for an elderly gentleman. She looked up from what she was doing and smiled at me.

"Hi Mia, I'll be right with you," Amanda said.

I looked over the menu board while I waited. The elderly gentleman paid for his drink when it was done and left. He was one of those people that you don't know but look vaguely familiar when you live in a small town, so I nodded at him as he left.

"Amanda, how are you this morning?" I asked.

"I'm fine," she said. "I have to tell you something."

I stepped up to the front counter and leaned closer to Amanda. She put her arms on top of the counter and leaned toward me.

"I hate to gossip, but this is gossip," she said. "When Brian and I were leaving Hank's Barbeque Shack, we drove by the Silver Dollar Bar and we saw the mayor's wife, Susan Goodall, standing out front kissing someone."

I looked at her. "Really? What kind of kiss was it? A friendly, 'I'll see you later' kiss, or an 'I really want to see you later' kiss?"

"The latter," she whispered. "It was weird considering her husband just died."

"Did you recognize the man?" I asked.

She shook her head. "No, I couldn't get a look at him. There was a car driving behind us and Brian didn't want to slow down so I could get a better look."

"That is odd," I said with a sigh. "You're sure it was a romantic kiss?"

"I wouldn't kiss anyone but Brian like that. Sorry, I probably shouldn't have said anything," she said. "Can I get you a coffee?"

"Yeah, a pumpkin latte," I said. "You know, Susan Goodall was kind of, well, for lack of a better word, 'loose' when we were in school. Maybe she never changed her ways."

"Maybe. Or maybe she was glad to be rid of her husband," she said, pouring coffee into a cup for me.

"Did you hear Fagan was arrested yesterday? I haven't spoken to Samantha to see if she was able to bail him out."

"Before I saw Mrs. Goodall kissing that man last night, Fagan was first on my list of possible suspects," she said. "Now Susan has moved up to the number one spot."

"I've been back and forth as to whether Fagan was the killer. I don't know about Susan though. She's been drunk in public a couple of times and now this," I said. "I wish everyone would go back to being normal around here."

"You can say that again," Amanda said. She squirted whipped cream onto my latte and handed it to me.

"It doesn't help that half the town is freaked out about some imaginary curse. It's been spreading to the tourists, too, " I said, searching in my purse for my debit card. I had last used it at the gas station and I was forever tossing it into my purse instead of putting it somewhere I could find it.

"A curse?" Amanda said. "That's silly. Why would there be a curse—"

"What?" I asked, finally locating the card and running it through the card reader.

"I suddenly remembered something my grandmother told me. She said there was a curse on Pumpkin Hollow that would suddenly become active every now and then. I forget how often she said it was. Maybe twenty or thirty years?"

"Seriously? Did your grandmother know Lisa's grandmother?" I asked.

She giggled. "I know it's silly. I remember being nine or so and she was so serious about it. She told me never to cross the creek down by the haunted farmhouse during a storm."

"What?" I said. "What does that have to do with anything?"

She shrugged. "I don't know. But she told me about it and it freaked me out. I was a kid, you understand. I didn't know much of anything about anything. I forgot all about that."

I shook my head. "The crazy things you hear around here. Thanks for the latte. I better get back to the shop."

"I'll see you later. Oh, let me know if you hear anything new about Fagan or the murder."

"I will," I said and left the coffee shop. I took a sip of my coffee and a drop of rain hit my nose. I looked up at the darkening sky. The clouds made the warm day feel humid.

Sultry. A sultry day is a day when evil is afoot.

That's what my grandmother called this kind of weather.

Chapter Twenty

I had intended to go straight home after work that evening, but at the last minute I made a left turn instead of a right. I headed toward the old haunted farmhouse and parked in front. It was a Wednesday and it wouldn't open again until Friday evening. I got out of my car and headed toward the charred remains of the corn maze.

The entire place was deserted except for the horses already put in the barn for the night. I kicked at the blackened ground with one booted foot. Dark clouds gathered together overhead, but I could still smell smoke beneath the smell of the threatening rain.

I caught a shadow out of the corner of my eye and I turned toward it. Jerry Crownover was standing in front of the barn. He smiled and walked toward me when I turned to face him.

"Hello Mia, what are you doing here?" he asked me when he got closer. His hair was uncombed and his shirt hanging out from his waistband.

I forced myself to smile. "I guess I'm mourning the loss of an important part of the Halloween season. What are you doing here, Jerry?"

He shrugged. "I guess you could say I was mourning Stan. I don't know why, but I guess I felt like I needed to come out here. It makes me feel closer to him. Has Ethan said how the murder investigation is going? You're seeing Ethan, aren't you?"

Something about the way he looked at me gave me the chills. "No, he hasn't mentioned much of anything about the murder investigation," I lied. I didn't like being out here alone with Jerry and I didn't like him bringing up my relationship with Ethan. I resisted the temptation to put my hand in the pocket that held my phone. And then I realized it wasn't there, anyway. I had left it in my purse that was now locked in the trunk of my car in the parking lot.

"That's a shame. I heard they arrested Fagan Branigan. I suppose we can all relax now. The killer's been caught."

"I would think they're keeping your sister apprised of how the investigation is going," I said. "Hasn't she talked to you about it?" I was pretty sure I could make a run for my car if I needed to. My ankle had healed up nicely.

He narrowed his eyes at me. "I suppose I could talk to her about it. What are you doing out here?"

"I already told you," I reminded him.

He nodded and stared at me. "I guess I'll get going now. I've got business to attend to."

"Have a nice evening," I said and watched him walk back toward the barn. I hadn't seen a car when I pulled up. A few minutes after he disappeared behind the barn, I heard a vehicle start up. I waited and saw him tear out onto the highway. He drove a white pickup and he stared at me longer than was safe as he pulled away. I wouldn't have thought Jerry, a businessman, would drive a pickup.

I let the breath out that I didn't know I was holding. I had never cared for Jerry but he had never creeped me out like he had just done. I watched the highway for several minutes after the truck disappeared.

I turned and headed toward the area where we had found the mayor's body, wondering if vital evidence had gone up in smoke along with the maze. The police had searched, but had they found everything? Probably not, since they had wanted to search one more time.

I didn't believe Jerry for one minute when he said he was mourning Stan and felt drawn here. There was a reason he was here, and I was pretty sure I knew what that reason was. I wondered if he had dug around in the dirt, looking for anything left behind.

The ground was fire-blackened in the area where the mayor's body had lain. I could see boot prints in the dirt on the side of where the maze walls had stood, just like Ethan had said. There were a lot of prints in different sizes and I couldn't see how they picked out the boot prints as being suspicious. But I wasn't a detective, so what did I know? I couldn't tell that anyone had been digging around in the dirt in this area, but maybe Jerry had covered things up.

With the maze gone, I couldn't tell the precise spot we had found him, but I knew I was close. I walked around, keeping my eyes focused on the ground, and trying not to kick up too much soot. My tan boots quickly turned black and the hems of my jeans soon matched.

I picked up a small charred stick and squatted down, running the stick around in the dirt. What had gone through the killer's mind as they pulled the trigger? I couldn't fathom what it was that made a person kill another human. I moved the dirt around some more, then stood up.

I supposed we could reconstruct the straw maze by buying a couple loads of baled straw, but the corn maze was a goner. The fire put the actors out of work and cut off the funds the maze would have earned. I walked on toward the far corner of the burned-out site.

Beyond the maze was the pumpkin patch. Thankfully the fire was put out before the fire got to the pumpkins, and pumpkin picking would go on as planned. I wracked my brain, trying to come up with some new attraction that was easy to obtain, inexpensive, and that would draw people to the farmhouse. All I could come up with was a larger straw maze and that didn't appeal to me. We could build a separate straw maze and put the actors in it, but it had its limitations. If someone got scared in the corn maze and ran into the sides of the maze, there was little chance they would get hurt. Hitting a solid wall of straw bales would be a lot more painful.

I turned back to the charred ground and walked along the edges, keeping my eyes on the ground. The killer had to have set the mazes on fire to destroy evidence. But then I had to wonder why it wasn't done immediately. A charred body would have taken longer to identify and with a little luck, obliterate more evidence. I looked in the direction Jerry had gone. I needed to talk to Ethan.

I squatted back down again and ran the stick through the ashes. I unearthed a small rock and a dirt-caked pumpkin seed. Moving the stick through the dirt in another spot brought up a broken and partially melted plastic spoon. I stirred up the dirt in another spot and dug around in the ashes. I found a soot-covered lump, and I squinted my eyes. *What was that?*

I picked it up and shook off the dirt and ashes. My eyebrows drew together as I tried to remember something. I had seen the item before. Then it came back to me. I stood up and shook it, then rubbed it against my jeans. I inhaled deeply, tucked it into my pocket and ran to my car.

Chapter Twenty-one

I parked my car in front of the candy shop and jumped out, slamming the door behind me. I felt the outside of my pocket, making sure the item I had dug up was still there.

When I pushed the candy shop door open, Mom was behind the counter, placing the leftover unsold candy into a bag. It was a few minutes before closing and the shop was empty of customers.

"Mia, why are you back? I thought you were going home to start dinner?" Mom asked me.

My eyes went to Andrea, sweeping the floor near the front window.

"I was. But then I forgot something," I said.

Andrea looked at me and smiled. Her eyes went to my sooty boots and the smile faded from her face.

"Hey, Mia, where have you been?" she asked, holding the broom still.

I steadied my breathing before answering. "I stopped off at the corn maze. I had an idea for another attraction, and I went to see if I could visualize it."

"Oh?" she asked. "What kind of attraction?" Her eyes met mine and she pulled the broom once more across the floor and glanced at my boots again.

I forced myself to smile. "Nothing. When I got there, I realized it was silly and it would never work."

"What kind of attraction? Maybe I can help you figure out something that would make it work?" she asked, taking a step toward me.

I saw Mom move over to the side counter and begin wiping the top with a dishcloth.

I shrugged. "It was silly. I'd feel dumb for even mentioning it."

Andrea smiled at me and glanced at my boots again. "You must have been working on figuring out how it would work."

"I'm sorry, I'm making a mess of the floor and here you are, trying to sweep it clean."

"It's not a problem. Go on, tell me about the new attraction," she coaxed.

"Well, if you insist," I said with a smile. "Goat tying." I had no idea where the idea came from, but I was thankful it showed up when it did.

Her brows knit together. "Goat tying?" she asked, and brought the broom across the floor in front of her.

"You know, like in the rodeos. Little kids chase a goat until they catch it and pull a ribbon from its tail. I told you it was silly," I said and took two steps forward and looked in my mother's direction. She didn't look up from her cleaning.

"Oh, I've seen that on TV," she said, nodding. "Why did you decide it wouldn't work?"

I looked down at my boots, then looked at her and smiled again. "Because what parent is going to want their kids running around in all that ash and then dragging it home with them on their shoes? After I'd walked around in it a few minutes, I realized the ash would be a problem. Sorry, I didn't mean to leave tracks on the floor."

She chuckled. "I can see your point. I guess we're stuck with all that ash there for a while. It would ruin just about any attraction or activity we tried to put in there, wouldn't it?"

I nodded. "It sure would. Here, hand me that broom and I'll clean up after myself." I held my hand out for it and she handed it to me.

"I'll just clean up in the kitchen," she said as she passed my mother.

"Okay, Andrea, I'm about finished over here," Mom said absently.

I hurried over to the counter to speak to my mother.

"Mom," I whispered. "Let's go home. Now."

She looked up at me. "I'm almost done here. I'll just be a couple more minutes."

"Now," I said and pulled out the pin from my pocket. I held it up for her to see. It was still covered in soot, but the jack-o-lantern face was clearly visible.

"What's that?" she asked, squinting at it.

I opened my mouth to answer her when Andrea appeared from the back room. Her hands were shaking as her fingers wrapped around a handgun.

"Andrea," I whispered.

"Why did you have to go looking?" she asked, slowly shaking her head. "Why couldn't you leave things alone?"

"What are you talking about?" I asked. If I played dumb, maybe we could get out of this.

"Don't play stupid," she said. "If you would have minded your own business, everything would have been okay."

Mom looked from me to Andrea, and then to the gun in her hands. "Andrea, what are you doing? Put that thing away before someone gets hurt."

"I'm sorry, Mrs. Jordan. I really am. You and your family have been so good to me. But we need to get in your car and go for a drive."

Mom and I stood rooted to the spot. I could see Mom trying to piece things together in her mind.

"Now!" Andrea shouted. Tears rolled down her cheeks and she motioned toward the door with the gun.

"Andrea, you don't have to do this," I pleaded. "We can work this out."

"Mia, don't argue with me. Don't make this harder than it has to be. Please," she said. She may have been crying, but there was an edge to her voice I hadn't heard before.

I nodded at my mother and we walked slowly toward the door. The self-defense course I took in college had taught me not to go anywhere with someone who had a gun, but my mother was in the line of fire and I couldn't bring myself to try anything that might get her hurt.

"I need to lock the shop door," I said when we were out on the sidewalk. I turned back toward the shop.

"Leave it be. It doesn't matter what happens to the shop," she said, stepping between me and the door. "Get in the car."

I had the keys to my car in my pocket and I fished them out. I had slipped the pin into my other pocket for safekeeping. Andrea may have wanted to end our lives, but I wasn't going down without a fight if I could help it, and I needed the pin as evidence.

I got behind the wheel of my car and Mom got into the passenger seat. Andrea sat in the back seat with the gun trained on us. My mind raced, trying to come up with something to do to stop her.

Chapter Twenty-two

A ndrea instructed me to drive out to the haunted farmhouse. My mind churned with ideas to get out of this situation, but most of the ideas I had involved me running away in a zigzag pattern so she couldn't hit me. Unfortunately, that left my mom. If I yelled, 'Mom, run in a zigzag pattern so she can't hit us', would she understand me? Or would she hesitate, not understanding what I had just said because of the fear she was feeling, thereby giving Andrea enough time to shoot her?

"Why are we going to the haunted farmhouse?" I asked. I felt a need to keep her talking. It might distract her and it would help keep the dark thoughts swirling through my mind from freaking me out. I needed to keep my wits about me.

"I don't know, it just seems like a good idea," she said from the backseat.

"What do you mean it seems like a good idea?" I asked, glancing in my rearview mirror. "What are we going to do there? Why don't we go talk to Ethan? He'll know how to handle things."

"Stop talking!" she shouted. "You're confusing me!"

I bit my lower lip. There went my plan to keep her distracted.

"Andrea, why don't we pull over and we can talk about this?" my mother suggested. She sounded much calmer than I felt and I glanced over at her.

"There's nothing to talk over. I did it. I killed the mayor. And now that you two know it was me, I have to get rid of you. I'm sorry, but I have to do it. I have no other choice."

"You're not making sense," Mom said. "We had no idea you killed the mayor. You're the last person we would suspect."

I slowed down and pulled into the haunted farmhouse parking lot. If I burned rubber and turned donuts in the dirt, could I knock Andrea over in the backseat? Maybe she would drop the gun and I could slam on the brakes and Mom and I could run.

"Pull over by the barn," Andrea said.

"What are you going to do?" I asked her. I needed a plan and I needed one now.

"Just do what I say," she said.

I could hear a quiver in her voice and it gave me hope. Andrea wasn't a coldblooded killer, in spite of having admitted she killed the mayor. She was a sweet college girl. I thought she was just scared enough that I might be able to get the advantage over her.

I pulled up and parked in front of the barn door and shut the engine off. My cell phone was in my pocket and I wondered how I could get to it without her noticing.

"Both of you get out of the car and stand in front of it with your hands where I can see them. Leave your doors open and don't try anything," she said, sounding calmer.

I glanced at Mom. Her face was white and her hand trembled as she reached for the door handle, but other than that, she seemed calm. I opened my car door and got out, leaving it open. I walked to the front of my car and turned toward Andrea as she slid out of the back seat on my side of the car.

"Open the barn door," she said to me, nodding toward it. The gun in her hand shook slightly and I hoped she wouldn't accidently pull the trigger. I needed more time to come up with a plan.

I moved slowly, afraid I would startle her. I pulled on the barn door and it swung open freely. The smell of hay and leather filled my nostrils and I inhaled, trying to calm my nerves. One of the horses stirred in its stall and snorted.

I looked at Andrea over my shoulder.

"Go inside. Both of you," she said, keeping her distance behind us as we entered the barn.

I looked at Mom as she came closer to me.

"Stop," Andrea said.

We stopped walking and turned toward her. We were in the middle of the barn. The clouds had parted and the sunlight streamed in through the open barn door, but it was the only source of light. If I ducked into a corner, would she be able to see me? It still left Mom as a sitting target for her. If Mom hesitated even a second, Andrea would have an easy shot.

"Andrea, please, let's talk this over," Mom said gently. The sound of her voice broke my heart. Mom was a gentle soul and seeing someone holding a gun on her felt like someone had reached in and grabbed hold of my heart and squeezed.

Andrea didn't answer my mother. She stood with the gun, still visibly shaking. She didn't want to kill us. I knew that much.

"Andrea, why did you kill the mayor?" I asked, trying to sound friendly.

She bit her lower lip before answering. "Because he stole the glee club money and got away with it. We couldn't go to regionals, so I missed out on getting a scholarship. I was so close. Why did he have to be so greedy?"

I tried to remember exactly how many years it had been since that had happened. Three? Four? Andrea could hold a grudge.

"Andrea, you're such a wonderful singer. You're going to make it even without a scholarship," I pointed out.

"I needed that scholarship to go away to school. I wanted to apply to a music school. But instead, I'm going to community college," she said bitterly.

Her parents shop was struggling and they didn't have the money to pay for an expensive music college. It had to be a bitter twist to have her dream stolen from her when she most likely would have been accepted if she had a scholarship.

"Andrea, let's sit down and talk about this sensibly," my mother suggested. She took a step toward her and Andrea held the gun up, aiming it at my mother's face.

I gasped.

"Stop!" I cried. "Don't do this, Andrea!"

She looked at me with tears in her eyes. "I don't have a choice."

Chapter Twenty-three

"Stop, Andrea!" I cried. "Don't do it. If you'll just calm down, we can think this thing through."

She aimed the gun at me. "There's nothing to talk about. I killed the mayor. Do you think the police will just let that go? There's no way to fix this."

"But you don't need to make it worse by shooting us," I said. "Maybe Ethan can help."

Tears streamed down her cheeks. "I had so many dreams. I was going to be somebody. That thief stole my dreams along with the money."

"Andrea, was it worth killing him over?" I asked. "Why did you kill him four years later?"

She shook her head slowly. "I didn't plan to. He texted me. He told me he wanted to see me to make up for what he did. He said to meet him out here at the corn maze. It made me so angry. I stole my dad's gun, but I didn't intend to kill him. I didn't trust him and I just wanted to protect myself."

"What do you mean?" I asked her. "Why would he text you? Why did he have your phone number?"

Tears were streaming down her face. "I worked in the mayor's office for two months last summer. He came on to me. I told him I wasn't interested, but he wouldn't leave me alone. I don't want to kill the two of you."

"Why didn't you just tell him no?"

"He promised he would help me get another scholarship. He said there was a program for interns and if he wrote a letter of recommendation, I would be guaranteed to get a scholarship. He said he wanted to talk to me in private and no one would see us out here when it was dark."

I wanted to tell her that meeting him out here in the dark did not have the makings of arranging for a scholarship, but I refrained from saying anything.

"Did he hurt you?" Mom asked gently.

She shook her head. "He tried. When I was in glee club in school, he tried to come on to me. That's why I brought the gun. Just in case. He said he wanted to get closer to me, and he put his arm around me, pulling me close. I could smell his stinking breath in my face. When I shoved him away, he grabbed me and tried to kiss me, holding me so tightly. I screamed and tried to push him away. I don't even remember taking the gun from my purse, but the gun went off before I knew what happened."

"You don't have to kill us," Mom said. "We can go to the police and tell them he tried to hurt you, and you got scared. We can tell them you wanted to tell the police, but you were too scared."

"It was self-defense, Andrea," I said, without bringing up the fact that she had shot him six times. If she was telling the truth, she may indeed have emptied the gun without realizing it.

She shook her head. "I can't. They won't believe me. I have to do this," she said and raised the gun to point at me again.

"You know the police will figure out it was you. What will you do with our bodies?" I asked. "You can't get away with this."

"I'll have to leave town," she said with a shrug. "I don't have a choice."

It was now or never. I hurled my keys with all the strength I had, hitting Andrea in the face. I had been on the softball team in high school and I had a mean fastball. She screamed and turned her back to me, bringing her free hand to her face.

"Run, Mom!" I screamed and sprinted down a dark corridor between the stalls.

"Come back here!" Andrea yelled.

I realized Mom wasn't running behind me. I glanced back, but she was nowhere to be seen, so I kept going. The corridor was a dead end unless I opened the back door to the barn. But then she would know where I went, so I grabbed a steel hay hook and crouched down in the dark. I could hear scuffling footsteps and I prayed Mom had gotten out or found a good place to hide. I was relieved when the footsteps came closer. Andrea was searching for me.

A light came on and the corridor was filled with light. I crouched down in the still dim corner and waited.

When she got closer, I jumped out hit her in the head with the backside of the steel hay hook. She screamed in pain and dropped the gun. I dived for it, snatching it up while she held onto her head and cried.

"Andrea, I wish you wouldn't have done this," I said.

Chapter Twenty-four

Mom sat sideways on the driver's seat of my car, with the door open. She sipped from a bottle of water, looking as calm as could be. But I knew the strained look on her face. She was shaken.

"Are you okay?" Ethan asked me after first checking on my mother. I was leaning on an old wooden wagon in front of the barn while several police officers searched the barn.

I nodded. I held my own bottle of water, but had no interest in it. "I'm okay."

His eyes met mine and I bit my lower lip to keep from crying.

"I'm glad you didn't get hurt," he said and glanced at the ambulance pulling away with Andrea in the back. I had hit her hard and her head had been bleeding, but she never lost consciousness. She had sobbed bitterly while I held the gun on her and we waited for the police. I wanted to cry with her. Andrea's life would be wasted behind bars.

"I'm glad neither of us were hurt," I said. "I can't help but feel sad about Andrea. She was one of the nicest people. At least I thought she was. She said she defended herself after Stan tried to hurt her. I believe it. I just don't know why she didn't tell the police what happened. Or why she went out to meet him in the dark. Scholarship or not, it wasn't worth it."

He nodded. "That would have been the smart thing to do. It's going to be hard to convince a judge it was self-defense when she takes two people hostage and plans to kill them. How did you know she killed Stan?"

I sighed. "I didn't at first. But I came out here to have a look around. While digging in the burned out corn maze, I came across this," I said. I dug into my pocket and pulled out the pin I had found earlier.

He held his hand out and I put the pin in his hand. He turned it over, examining it. "What's this?"

"Andrea made these jack-o-lantern pins and gave one to me, Mom, and Lisa. She told me she also made one for herself, but I never saw her wear it. When I found this one in the dirt near the maze, I didn't know for sure it belonged to her, but I had a bad feeling about it. It looked nearly identical to the ones she made for the rest of us. She was closing the store with my mother, so I rushed back to the shop. She saw the soot on my boots and she knew where I'd been."

"She just assumed you knew?" he asked, brushing my hair out of my face.

"I guess I must have looked a little freaked out when I realized Andrea had been at the corn maze. Everyone knew she still held a grudge against Stan about the missing glee club funds. I thought my mother might be in danger and I guess she read it on my face and put two and two together."

Ethan smiled sadly. "Keeping a secret like that would put a person on edge, just waiting for someone to figure out the truth. It's a shame she threw her life away. She's so young and talented. Maybe the judge will go easy on her, but I don't have a lot of confidence in that."

"I don't either," I said.

"I have news," he said.

"What?"

"Jerry Crownover was picked up a little while ago with a couple cans of gasoline in the bed of his truck, along with some rags and propane lighters."

"What do you mean?" I asked.

"He was speeding down the highway, driving recklessly. He had a couple of beers in him, so he was arrested and brought downtown. When the arresting officer saw what he had in his truck, he started questioning him. He denied it at first, but then he broke down and said he had come out here to burn down the farmhouse."

"Why would he do that? Did he burn the mazes, too?" I asked, trying to put this together. When I had seen Jerry earlier, I was sure he had killed Stan. I had dug around in the dirt, thinking I would find something to incriminate him that I could take to Ethan. Instead, I found the pin.

Ethan nodded. "He thought the fire would spread to the farmhouse, but the fire department put it out before that happened. He's the person that bought the farmhouse a few years ago. He kept it a secret and took a large insurance policy out on it. He came back this evening to finish the job, but you were here."

"Oh," I said. "That's why he was acting strange. He really made me nervous."

I sighed and looked at my mother. Tears filled my eyes. If Andrea had killed her, I would never have forgiven her and I wouldn't forgive myself for not rescuing her. I was thankful Andrea went after me when we ran. Mom had told me she ran and hid behind some bales of hay in the barn. She would have been a sitting duck if Andrea had gone after her.

"I guess I better get Mom home. I'm suddenly feeling exhausted and I know she's tired, too."

He nodded. "Stress does that to you."

"Oh, I forgot we left the shop door unlocked. I'll have to stop by there first."

"Give me the key and I'll take care of it. I'll drop the key back by later this evening," he offered.

I smiled. "Thanks. I'd appreciate that."

I handed him the key and looked at him before turning back to Mom. Ethan was a great guy and I was glad he was in my life.

He leaned over and kissed me. "I'm glad you weren't hurt."

I nodded. "Me too."

Pumpkin Hollow may not have been the same town I remembered from my childhood, but I still loved it. And in spite of the trouble we'd experienced the last few weeks, I was glad I had moved home. Otherwise, I might not have become reacquainted with Ethan. And that would have been a real tragedy.

Author's Note

I'M HAVING A LOT OF fun writing about Mia and Pumpkin Hollow. When I was a little girl, I loved Halloween, as most children do. I remember being a pink elephant, a blue bunny, and a green ghost, among other costumes. My mother kept the boxes of holiday decorations in a storage room that we kids weren't usually allowed to enter. The fall day we came home from school to see the Halloween boxes sitting outside the door of that storage room was a happy day! The boxes held costumes from past years along with decorations. I feel like I get to relive those days through these books.

Book three of Pumpkin Hollow is coming the summer of 2018. Thanks for reading!

Made in the USA
Lexington, KY
11 December 2019